MW01248521

by

Kathi Daley

This book is a work of fiction. Names, characters, places, and incidents either are products of the author's imagination or are used fictitiously. Any resemblance to actual events or locales or persons, living or dead, is entirely coincidental.

Copyright © 2016 by Katherine Daley

Version 1.0

All rights reserved, including the right of reproduction in whole or in part in any form.

I want to thank the very talented Jessica Fischer for the cover art.

I so appreciate Bruce Curran, who is always ready and willing to answer my cyber questions.

And, of course, thanks to the readers and bloggers in my life, who make doing what I do possible.

Thank you to Randy Ladenheim-Gil for the editing.

Special thanks to Joanne Kocourek, Elaine Robinson, Vivian Shane, and Nancy Farris, for submitting recipes.

And finally I want to thank my sister Christy for always lending an ear and my husband Ken for allowing me time to write by taking care of everything else.

Books by Kathi Daley
Come for the murder, stay for the romance.

Zoe Donovan Cozy Mystery:
Halloween Hijinks
The Trouble With Turkeys
Christmas Crazy
Cupid's Curse
Big Bunny Bump-off
Beach Blanket Barbie
Maui Madness
Derby Divas
Haunted Hamlet
Turkeys, Tuxes, and Tabbies
Christmas Cozy
Alaskan Alliance
Matrimony Meltdown
Soul Surrender
Heavenly Honeymoon
Hopscotch Homicide
Ghostly Graveyard
Santa Sleuth
Shamrock Shenanigans
Kitten Kaboodle
Costume Catastrophe – *August 2016*

Whales and Tails Cozy Mystery:

Romeow and Juliet
The Mad Catter
Grimm's Furry Tail
Much Ado About Felines
Legend of Tabby Hollow
Cat of Christmas Past
A Tale of Two Tabbies
The Great Catsby
Count Catula – *September 2016*
Cat of Christmas Present – *November 2016*

Seacliff High Mystery:

The Secret
The Curse
The Relic
The Conspiracy
The Grudge

Sand and Sea Hawaiian Mystery:

Murder at Dolphin Bay
Murder at Sunrise Beach
Murder at the Witching Hour – *September 2016*

Road to Christmas Romance:
Road to Christmas Past

Tj Jensen Paradise Lake
Pumpkins in Paradise – Sept. 2016
Snowmen in Paradise – Sept 2016
Bikinis in Paradise – Sept 2016
Christmas in Paradise – Sept 2016
Puppies in Paradise – Sept 2016
Halloween in Paradise – Sept 2016
Treasure in Paradise – April 2017

Chapter 1

Monday, June 20

This could just not get any worse. If the gates of hell opened up and swallowed me whole it wouldn't be worse.

"So what do you think?" My mother beamed at me.

What did I think? My fifty-eight-year-old mother was standing in front of me in a tiny see-through negligee that even I wouldn't wear. Don't get me wrong: My mother is in excellent shape for her age, but not only has she had five children, she's had five Catholic children. My mom is not just a little religious, she's totally committed to the Church and serves as both the head of the St. Patrick's Women's Bible Study and the Women's Guild. It just doesn't seem right that my very Madonnalike mother is parading around in the "naughty" store, wearing the skimpy outfit she plans to wear on her wedding night to a man who may very well turn out to be Satan himself.

"Caitlin Hart, are you listening to me?"

"Yeah, I'm listening."

"So what do you think of the negligee I picked out?"

"Aren't you afraid you'll be cold?"

"It's June."

"But still chilly at night. Maybe something in a nice floor-length gown. Flannel is always nice at this time of year."

My mom looked directly at me and put her hands on her hips. "Would you wear floor-length flannel on your wedding night?"

"I might," I defended myself, even though I knew that was a lie. "It's just that you're…"

"Old?"

"Maternal. You've been married before. Do you really need to go all-out this time around?"

My mom twirled around, showing off way too much of her derriere. "I most certainly do need to go all-out." She looked at me with a softer expression. "Your dad has been gone for a long time."

I knew she was right, and I wasn't even against the notion of her moving on, but the man she was engaged to was definitely not the man I wanted my mother tied to for the rest of her life. For one thing, he was arrogant and opinionated. He made it clear he thought the Harts to be country hicks who wouldn't know a 1996 Boërl & Kroff brute from a 2016 Korbel Brut. Okay, maybe he had a point with that one, but life was about more than expensive champagne and even more expensive cars. It was about friends and family and planting roots that endured from one generation to the next.

"Cait?"

"It's nice, Mom." I hated the look of uncertainty on her face, but even more I hated the fact that she was leaving Madrona Island and, more importantly, leaving *us* after living here her entire life.

"Maybe it is a bit much. And it's expensive. I don't suppose the cost is justified when I know it probably will be shreds of fabric on the floor within seconds."

Geez, how did I draw the short straw? My siblings and I had divvied up the unpleasant tasks associated with the wedding so that none of us would be burdened with them all. My eldest brother Aiden has been coerced into walking my mom down the aisle, even though I knew he'd rather walk on glass, my older sister Siobhan was going to act as maid of honor, my brother Danny was in charge of the music, and I ended up with dress and trousseau shopping. My younger sister Cassidy was so traumatized that we'd decided to let her off the hook completely.

"No," my mom decided after walking back and forth in front of the mirror several dozen times, "you only get married once, or maybe twice in life, and I want to look the best I can. I'm buying it. I need to pick up a few other things as well."

"I'll just wait for you out front."

"Okay. When we're done here we can go look at flowers."

"Siobhan has flowers. I have cake."

"Does it matter?"

"No." I sighed. "I guess not."

I headed toward the front of the store and fresh air while my mom changed back into her street clothes. I wanted her to be happy, I really did; I just didn't happen to think that the extravagant Reginald Pendergrass was the one to make her happy in the long run. For one thing, what was up with that name? If I was named Reginald you could bet I'd go by Naldy or Reggie, but no, Reginald considered it a mortal sin if you called him by anything but his full name. And then there was the fact that he had expensive taste and appeared to have a lot of money yet he seemed to be forever forgetting his wallet.

Aiden, who takes care of my mom's finances, shared that Mom had blown through a good chunk of her savings since she'd been dating the man. That made all of us suspicious. I mean, what did we really know about the guy? Mom had met him on a cruise, and then a few months later she'd announced that she was betrothed to this man she barely knew and we had just met. What was with all the rush?

"Hey, Cait," Val Corning, my friend from high school, greeted me. "Why are you loitering out here in front of the naughty store?"

"I'm waiting for my mom."

"I heard she was getting hitched. Good for her. And good for owning her sexuality and shopping at the store no one else in town will admit to entering, even though they manage to stay in business just fine."

"Yeah, it's great," I muttered sarcastically. "Just what every daughter wants, to go to the naughty store with her mother."

"Speaking of naughty, did you hear that Alex Turner is back in town?"

"Yeah, I heard." Alex was a friend of mine whom I'd first met the previous December, when his biological father had hired me to find him. It's a rather long story, but basically, Alex had been kidnapped as a baby and his father had spent a lifetime wondering what had become of him. The uncertainty had made him a bitter old man intent on spreading misery wherever he went. I wanted to save an apartment building he was going to tear down, so I made a deal with him to look for his son if he would save the structure. At the time, Alex was this sweet guy, without a rotten bone in his body, but it seemed that wealth hadn't been kind to him; he'd returned to Madrona Island after college let out for the summer with an uppity attitude and a group of equally unpleasant friends who were all staying in the oceanfront mansion his father, Balthazar Pottage, had given him.

"Have you heard about the parties he's been throwing?" Val asked. "Talk about totally legendary. When I met the guy last December I thought he was a babe, but he seemed sort of boring. You know what I mean?"

"I do." And I did. The old Alex was awesome; the new Alex not so much.

"Not at all the type to throw the opulent parties he's been known to host since he's been home. And it's not just the food and the booze; his guest list is very exclusive. You have to be pretty lucky to get an invite. My friend Stephanie and I have been trying to get in for weeks with absolutely no luck. And by Madrona Island standards we're popular. I feel like I need to up the ante and prove I'm worthy of hanging out with the rich kids. I may have to spend my entire savings on a new wardrobe, but it will be worth it. Don't you think?"

"I guess if you like that sort of thing."

"Oh, I do. I really, really do. I don't suppose you could put in a good word for me? I know you're friends with Alex, and maybe between the wardrobe and a recommendation from you I'll actually get through the front door."

"I'm not sure I can help you. Alex and I really haven't hung out all that much since he's been home."

"But if you do see him you'll ask?"

"Sure." I doubted I'd be chatting with Alex any time soon, but agreeing seemed the easiest way to end the conversation, which was just making me sad.

"Thanks. I appreciate it. I'd do just about anything to hook up with Alex's friend Nick. Have you seen that guy? Talk about a babe. If you ask me, he's the brains behind the whole thing. You know he's from old money? If I had to guess

Nick has taught Alex everything he knows about living the rich lifestyle."

"I had the same impression."

"Talk about luck. Alex might be the same old boring guy with good looks but little else going for him if not for Nick."

"Yeah." I almost felt like I wanted to cry for the old Alex I'd loved and enjoyed being around. "Luck."

"I should go. My boyfriend is waiting for me at the deli down the street. Now don't forget to speak to Alex for me."

I just smiled. The entire conversation was more than just a little depressing. I was still having a hard time coming to grips with the fact that a perfectly nice guy could turn into such a jerk in such a short amount of time. They say money changes people, and for the first time I really believed that was true.

"Was that Val Corning?" my mom asked when she joined me on the sidewalk outside the store.

"Yeah, that was Val." I took my mom's bag and started toward the car. The quicker we got out of here the better as far as I was concerned.

"Such a nice girl. I can't remember why you stopped hanging out with her."

I shrugged as I opened the passenger door for Mom. "People change. We grew up and grew apart. Are you ready to head home?"

"The flowers. We can't forget the flowers."

"Oh, right. The flower shop it is."

"I'm sure it wasn't that bad," my best friend, Tara O'Brian, commented later that afternoon when I returned to work at Coffee Cat Books, the coffee bar/bookstore/cat lounge we owned. Now that the weather had warmed and the whales had returned to the area, business had been brisk, but as chance would have it, there was a brief lull in the day we used to stock shelves and catch up.

"Trust me, it was. Fifty-eight-year-old women shouldn't be ordering rose petals to scatter on their bed. I thought I was going to die when Mom asked for them. Couldn't she just say they were for the flower girl or something?"

Tara laughed. "Your mom does seem to have reconnected with her youth."

"I don't think the youth she's connected to is her own. I'm pretty sure my mom didn't shop at the naughty store or ask the woman at the flower shop for rose petals to scatter on her bed the first time she was married."

"You can't know that," Tara countered. "You weren't around back then. You should ask Maggie. I bet she knows what your mom was like when she married your dad."

The last thing I wanted to do was ask my Aunt Maggie what my mom was like when she was young, especially since I'd found out that my very straitlaced aunt had been sleeping with the local priest when *she* was young. Okay, he wasn't a priest at the time, he was just her boyfriend, but still... You grow up with certain idealized views of the adults in your life only to find that the image of the person you thought you knew was no more than a mirage brought about by layers upon layers of expectations and false assumptions.

"How about we change the subject from my mother and the unwise choices she's making lately?"

"Fine by me," Tara said. "I went through the applications we received for summer help and picked out five people to interview. I think we should do it together. Is Thursday good for you?"

"Yeah." I sighed. "Whenever."

"Is there a problem?"

"I was just thinking about our last seasonal employee and how much I wish he was going to be with us this summer."

"Yeah," Tara agreed. "I miss him too. I really didn't expect Alex to come back to work for us once he found out he was the heir to millions, but I did expect to spend time with him as a friend. He's changed so much."

"Who's changed so much?" my sister Siobhan asked as she walked into the store in the middle of our discussion.

"Alex," I answered.

"Finn was telling me about some of the trouble he and his friends have been getting into. Not just here but even before they came to the island. I find it hard to believe it's even the same guy who was so sweet and played Santa for all the kids out of the goodness of his heart just a few short months ago."

"He's not the same guy." I nodded. "He's a totally different person. I was just thinking that money changes people, but it seems like the guy is almost possessed. It's creepy."

"Finn seems to think Alex's new friend is bad news. It seems he's been arrested a ton of times, but his dad has more money than God, so no matter what he does he finds a way to fix it. Finn said he thought after the last fiasco his dad was going to cut him off, but given the parties they've been having, it seems apparent he didn't follow through."

"I'm surprised Pottage hasn't cut Alex off," Tara contributed.

"I guess he figures he missed so much of his son's life, and they don't have a lot of years left together, so he doesn't want to fight," I theorized. "Balthazar Pottage is a very rich and very old man. I can understand why he would choose his battles."

Siobhan walked over to the coffee bar and poured herself a cup. "So how did shopping with Mom go?"

"Don't even ask," I grumbled.

"That bad?"

"Cait doesn't think a daughter should have to go to the adult lingerie store with her mother no matter what the occasion," Tara supplied when I didn't answer right away.

"Mom took you to the naughty store? I thought you were going shopping for her trousseau."

"We did. Trust me, you don't want the details."

"She didn't buy ... well, you know."

"Let's just say she came out of the store with a pretty big bag."

Siobhan made a face that mirrored what I felt. "Poor Cait. No daughter should have to know whatever it is you know—you know?"

"I know."

"I can't imagine why she dragged you along if her plan was to buy…well, you know."

"Can we change the subject?" I requested. "The entire situation makes me want to be sick."

"Sure, I'm sorry." Siobhan patted me on the shoulder. "How did it go with the bakery?"

"We didn't go to the bakery. Mom wanted to go pick out flowers instead."

"But I had flowers. You had cake and I had flowers. We agreed."

"I guess Mom doesn't understand our system. She insisted on doing the flowers today, even though I tried to explain that you had flowers. You can take her for cake."

"But I'm on a diet."

Tara started laughing. I mean really laughing.

"What's so funny?" I asked.

"The two of you make it sound like you're arguing over who has to babysit a child."

I sighed. "Lately I feel like Mom *is* a child."

"I'll agree your mom has been acting out of character lately, but she's still an adult. If you don't want to go on all these errands with her just explain that you're too busy. I'm sure she's capable of picking out a cake on her own. Besides, isn't that something Reginald should be doing with her?"

"My future stepdaddy is out of town and isn't planning to return until right before the wedding," I informed Tara.

"Really? He's making your mom handle everything by herself? That doesn't seem fair."

"Exactly."

Our conversation was interrupted by two women who came in for lattes and the new-release mysteries we'd recently gotten in. To be honest I was happy for the interruption. The subject of my mother and her impending nuptials was getting old fast. Mom had only just met Reginald in February and by April she'd called us all together to announce her engagement. Not only hadn't she known him long but Reginald lived in California, so Mom had actually spent very little time with him. We all thought that her hurrying in to marriage was a mistake, but she wasn't listening to anyone but the man who had captured her heart and put a ring on her finger.

"So the reason I popped in," Siobhan said to me after Tara went to help the customers, "was to ask if you're free tonight to talk about the shower."

"Shower?"

"Mom is expecting a bridal shower, and as her maid of honor she made it clear to me that it's my job to organize one. She gave me a guest list, but I could really use help with the rest. I thought maybe you and Cody could join Finn and me for dinner and we could come up with a plan."

"I'm free," I confirmed. "And I'm pretty sure Cody is as well, although I'm not overly thrilled with the idea of a shower. I keep hoping Mom will come to her senses and this whole nightmare will be over."

"She seems pretty committed to following through with her plans."

"Yeah. She really does. When and where?"

"Antonio's at seven?"

"We'll meet you there."

After Siobhan left I decided to go out onto the wharf, where we'd set up tables so our customers could enjoy the feel of the ocean during the warmer summer months. Large umbrellas offered shade during the heat of the day and portable heaters provided extra warmth during the chilly mornings.

"Excuse me." An adorable young girl with long brown hair and big blue eyes who looked to be about six or seven approached me.

"Yes?" I turned and looked toward her. "Can I help you with something?"

"My dog Ariel is lost. Have you seen her?"

The girl handed me a hand-drawn picture of a dog.

"Is this Ariel?" I asked.

"Yes. He's black with long hair and big eyes. He's my best friend and I have to find him."

"I absolutely understand." I looked around the wharf, which appeared to be devoid of adults. "Is you mother with you?"

"She's with God in heaven."

"I'm so sorry. How about your dad?"

"Sleeping. I'm supposed to be watching cartoons, but I miss Ariel so much. Have you seen her?"

I looked at the drawing again, which was little more than a stick figure. "I haven't seen her, but I'll be happy to help you look for her. My boyfriend owns the newspaper and I know he'd be happy to put Ariel's picture in the midweek edition, but as wonderful as your drawing is, we'll really need a regular photograph. Do you have one?"

"No, but my daddy might."

"How about we go ask him?"

"Okay."

"My name is Caitlin Hart, but most people just call me Cait. What's yours?"

"Rosalyn Dublin."

"Nice to meet you, Rosalyn. Just let me tell my friend what I'm doing and then we'll go talk to your dad to see what we can do."

I told Tara where I was going and walked the girl down the street to the Pelican Bay Inn. The door Rosalyn led me to was locked; I supposed it might have locked behind her when she left her room. I knocked on the door and waited.

"Yeah?" A man who looked to be half asleep answered. "Rosalyn, what are you doing out there? I told you to watch cartoons while I got some sleep."

"I was looking for Ariel."

He let out a long sigh of exhaustion. "You can't go off on your own whenever you want. We don't know people here like we do back home. Something bad could happen to you." The man looked up at me. "Thank you for bringing Rosalyn back."

"She said her dog is lost?"

"Yeah. We came over on the ferry last night and when Rosalyn opened the door to get back into the car Ariel got out. I tried to find her, but the ferry had just docked and everyone began to get off. I had to drive off because my car was blocking all the others behind me. I went back to see if I could find her after everyone disembarked, but there was no sign of her."

"It's a miracle she wasn't hit by a car."

"It really is, but we didn't find any sign that had occurred."

"We looked all around for her last night, but we can't find her." Rosalyn began to cry. "She doesn't know where we're staying while we wait for our house to be ready. How's she going to be able to find us?"

Rosalyn's dad pulled her into his arms. "We'll look some more today. I just needed to get some sleep. Yesterday was a very long day."

"My name is Cait," I introduced myself.

"Ben."

"My boyfriend owns the local paper. If you have a photo of Ariel I'm sure he'll be happy to run it free of charge."

"I do have some photos of Rosalyn with Ariel on my phone."

"I'll give you my e-mail address. If you e-mail a photo to me I'll have Cody print it in the paper, and I'll also make up some flyers to distribute around town. This is an island, so she can't have gotten too far. We'll find her."

Chapter 2

There comes a time in every adult's life when they find they've become the parent while their parent or parent figure has become the child. I just hadn't expected it to happen so soon to me. I mean really, I hadn't even had my own kids yet and I certainly didn't feel ready to take on such a huge responsibility, yet I seemed to constantly find myself in the position of parenting those around me. Tara thinks this is more about my need to parent than it is about the needs of those around me to be parented. Who knows; maybe she's right. I suppose I do have a tendency to want to manage the lives of those I care for, which in the end just makes me nuts.

"Thanks for picking me up," Cody said after he greeted me with a kiss. His car had broken down while he was out taking photos for the midweek edition of the *Madrona Island News* and had to be towed to the repair shop, so I'd picked him up at the paper and given him a ride home and then to dinner.

"No problem. Thanks for putting Ariel's photo on the front page of the paper."

"Nothing worse for a child than a lost pet."

"I put flyers around town as well. We'll find her. Do they know what's wrong with your car?"

"They think it's just the starter. It should be ready by tomorrow afternoon and the guy at the repair shop said he'd deliver it to the newspaper when it's ready, so if you can just give me a ride tonight and then back into town in the morning I should be good to go."

"Do you need to stop by your place before we go to dinner?"

"I'd like to change my clothes and I should bring Mr. Parsons something to eat as well. I know if I don't he'll just open a can of soup."

Mr. Parsons owned the house where Cody had an apartment on the third floor. Mr. Parsons was sort of a surrogate grandfather to Cody, who went out of his way to make sure he was happy and well fed.

"I'll call in an order to the diner and we can pick it up on the way," I offered. "Meat loaf with all the trimmings?"

"Yeah, he'll like that, but be sure to tell them to go easy on the potatoes and double up on the veggies. I'm afraid Mr. Parsons has put on some weight since his fall. I need to make more of an effort to make sure he gets the exercise he needs."

We picked up dinner and I sat and chatted with Mr. Parsons while Cody took a quick shower and changed his clothes. He didn't look overweight to me, but I realized Cody was just trying to make sure he was as healthy as possible during his final years.

"If you're going to Antonio's bring me back some cheesecake," Mr. Parsons requested.

"I thought Cody wanted you to watch your sugar intake."

"I ate all my vegetables. I deserve dessert."

"You fed your vegetables to Rambler." I pointed to Mr. Parsons's dog.

"You going to rat me out?"

"No, I'm not going to tell on you. I'll bring the cheesecake, but just a small piece, and next time eat your vegetables."

"Yes, Mother."

"I'm not your mother, but I do care about you, as does Cody, which is why we're constantly nagging you to take better care of yourself."

Mr. Parsons smiled. "I know. I don't really mind. But I still want the cheesecake."

"Don't worry; I'll bring you some."

"Did you have a nice day with your mother?" he asked.

I just groaned.

"I know you aren't thrilled with the way things are going, but your mother is a grown woman capable of making her own choices," Mr. Parsons reminded me.

"I know. You're the tenth person to tell me that today. I guess I should start listening to everyone and stop trying to control that which I clearly can't, despite how much this whole thing is totally freaking me out."

"Might be a good idea. I'd hate to see you damage your relationship with your mother over it."

"I know. You're right. From this minute forward I vow to let my mom do what she's going to do without interference from me."

"That's my girl."

It was amazing how much Mr. Parsons had changed since Cody'd moved in. There was a time all he would do was growl at me when I came by to check on him, but here he was giving me advice, and not just any advice but the good stuff. I felt comfortable with my vow to let Mom live her own life and determined to see it through. Of course that vow would only last until I arrived at the restaurant and heard Finn's news.

"What do you mean, Reginald Pendergrass doesn't exist?" I demanded.

"When it became apparent that your mother was serious about marrying this man, I decided to do a background check on him," Finn informed me. Ryan Finnegan was not only my sister Siobhan's boyfriend but a longtime friend of the family, so it made sense he'd be as concerned as we were. He was a deputy sheriff, so he had resources we didn't, and I appreciated his efforts. "I knew Siobhan was worried that your mother had barely met him before becoming engaged to him, and I had to agree that the timeline for this particular relationship seemed hurried at best. My initial inquiry for a Reginald Pendergrass of Newport Beach, California, failed to uncover any information on any such man, and I began to dig deeper. In all, I've found seventeen people named Reginald Pendergrass, and I've checked out each one of them and can now say I've eliminated them all. Of course I don't know that Reginald Pendergrass is the man's legal name, and I don't have the benefit of a social security number or even a birth date, so the fact that I haven't been able to find him living in California or even on the West Coast shouldn't be cause for alarm. Still, I do think we should get some additional information and dig a little deeper before your mother actually marries him."

I looked at Siobhan. She seemed as worried as I was. "What do you need to know?" I asked.

"A legal name, birthdate, driver's license, or social security number. Anything that will help narrow my search. If he were in town I'd suggest getting a peek at his driver's license, but he isn't, so we'll need to think of something else."

"You could just ask your mom." Cody turned from me to Siobhan.

"She'd have a fit if she found out we were investigating him," I said.

"Have they applied for a marriage license yet?" Finn wondered.

"I don't think so."

"Can you run his photo through facial recognition?" Siobhan asked Finn.

"I could, but I'm not confident it would turn up anything."

"What about the cruise line?" Cody suggested. "We know which ship your mom was on when she met him. Maybe the cruise line has a record of a passenger by that name and can give us a mailing address or some other way to locate him."

"It couldn't hurt to ask," Finn agreed. "I'll look into that tomorrow. In the meantime, if you find a way to slip subtle inquiries about Reginald into everyday conversation with your mother, I'd do so. Maybe you can pretend to want to mail him something as an excuse to ask for his address, or maybe you can pretend to want to add his birthday to your calendar as a way of gaining that information."

"Yeah, okay. I'll see what I can find out."

Siobhan contributed, "As things stand, I think we should go ahead with plans for Mom's shower. I know she's going to ask about it the next time we talk. It's only four weeks until the wedding."

"As much as I don't want to talk about anything to do with the wedding, I guess you're right," I said. "Where should we start?"

"Mom gave me a guest list. There are over a hundred women on it."

"A hundred?"

"Mom does know a lot of people. I guess the biggest challenge will be to find a venue to accommodate that many people."

I shrugged. "It's going to be hard to find something this close to the wedding."

"It occurred to me to have an outdoor shower. I'm sure Maggie would let us use her yard and it would be a lot less expensive. Besides, we won't need to worry about losing our deposit if Mom comes to her senses and cancels the wedding at the last minute."

"An outdoor shower would be nice as long as the weather holds," I agreed. "I think we should ask her about it, although we might need to consider alternate plans should it rain."

Siobhan and I spent the next twenty minutes discussing the various aspects of the party while Cody and Finn discussed the Seahawks' upcoming season. By the time our salad arrived we hadn't figured out much except for the fact that we didn't want to start putting deposits down until we found out who exactly it was Mom was engaged to. For now, we would simply plan but not purchase.

"Look who just walked in," Siobhan whispered as the waitress brought our main course.

I turned around to find Alex with his buddy Nick and a woman I knew only as Daisy with him. Although Alex had been a bit of a jerk lately, I didn't want to be rude, so I waved in his direction. He waved back and it looked like he might come over, which led Nick to say something that caused him to turn his back on us.

"What was that all about?" Siobhan asked.

"It seems to me Nick is somehow controlling Alex's actions. I don't know why and I don't know how, but every time I see the two of them together it seems Nick is making all the calls."

"If you want my opinion Nick is going to control Alex right into jail," Finn observed. "I'm pretty sure there are some legally questionable things going on at those parties they throw."

"I keep thinking I'll run into Alex someday when he's alone and talk to him," I commented, "but Nick always seems to be with him. I'm even thinking about going out to the island to talk to Balthazar Pottage. I know Alex is an adult and there really isn't a lot his father can do about his behavior, but I have a feeling Nick will disappear as quickly as he appeared if Alex's money suddenly dries up."

"I doubt Alex would welcome your interference in his life," Siobhan pointed out.

"Yeah, you're right. He can figure it out himself."

Even as I said that, I had this awful feeling that figuring it out wasn't going to be the case at all. Alex was an adult, and maybe he should be allowed to make his own choices, and my mother was an adult, and maybe she should be able to marry whoever she chose to without interference from her children, and Mr. Parsons was an adult, and maybe he should be able to eat cheesecake for dinner if he wanted to, but I cared about these people, which made it hard to stand back and watch as their decisions might cause their world to crash around them.

"Can I get any of you dessert?" the waitress asked.

"I'll have a piece of cheesecake to go," I ordered.

"After all that spaghetti?" Siobhan scolded.

"It's for later," I defended myself.

"It's for Mr. Parsons," Cody guessed.

"Yeah, it's for Mr. Parsons." I looked at Cody. "He wasn't sure you'd want him to have it, so I told him I'd sneak it."

"Mr. Parsons doesn't need my permission to have cheesecake. I go out of my way to make sure he eats healthy meals, but I've grown fond of the old goat and I feel the need to do what I can to keep him well."

"I know. And he knows too." I squeezed Cody's hand.

After we said our good-byes to Finn and Siobhan, Cody and I headed back toward the peninsula, where we both lived. "It's a beautiful night. Are you up for a walk on the beach?" I asked.

"Sounds good. Let's stop by to deliver Mr. Parsons's cheesecake first. We can pick up Rambler before we head over to your place so both dogs can have a walk."

"I'm sure Max will welcome the exercise. I'm afraid I've been pretty busy lately; we haven't gotten in as many morning runs as we usually do."

By the time we dropped off the cheesecake and picked up Rambler from Mr. Parsons's and Max from my cabin, it was completely dark and the moon had begun its ascent into the sky. Cody and I walked hand in hand as the dogs ran on the beach in front of us. It was a warm night, with barely a breeze to ripple the surface of the water as the small waves rolled gently onto shore.

"I never did have the chance to ask you about your trip to Tampa. How'd it go?"

Cody had been asked by the Navy to redesign the training for the SEAL program, and as part of that project he'd spent a week in Florida, meeting with the advisory team he was going to be working with. He'd come home on Saturday, but we'd both been busy and had had very little chance to talk.

"It was a productive trip. We talked through a lot of the issues and I think we're on the same page. The next phase of the project will require quite a bit of time on my part, but I'm hoping to have something for the group to consider when I go back to Tampa in the fall."

"You have another trip planned?"

"Just for a week. You should come with me."

"Maybe I will. I really missed you this last time."

Cody stopped walking. He turned and pulled me into his arms. "I missed you too. More than I can say."

I rested my head on his chest and listened to his heart beat. It was in these moments, when the world got quiet and it felt as if it was just the two of us on the planet, that I found myself wishing time would stop. Cody and I had been dating for over a year, and in the course of that time, I'd come to be sure he was the man I wanted to spend the rest of my life with. It's true that in the beginning I made it clear to Cody that I wasn't ready for marriage, babies, and joint funeral plots, but over the past few months I'd given our situation a lot of thought, and I'd decided maybe it was time for us to take the next step in our relationship.

The dilemma I faced now was how to let a man I'd quite clearly told I was *not* ready for a long-term commitment in the guise of a proposal know that after months of self-evaluation I was good to go. I suppose I could just come right out and tell Cody that my feelings had changed and let him know if he were to ask I would say yes, but somehow that seemed calculated and just a bit unromantic. I thought about dropping some subtle hints, but every time the subject of weddings came up lately it was in the context of my mother's, thus turning it into a negative topic. I supposed the best thing to do was to wait until after my mother was shackled to the monster she was marrying before I even entertained the subject of my own nuptials. After all, dealing with one Hart wedding at a time was about all I could handle. Of course I wouldn't be surprised if it wasn't long before Finn put a ring on Siobhan's finger again. In some ways I was surprised they weren't already engaged; perhaps, like me, they were waiting for the insanity of my mother's wedding to reach its logical conclusion.

Cody pulled away slightly. "We should get back."

"Do you want to stay over?"

"I'd love to, but I have some work to finish up tonight. Maybe tomorrow night. We can go to dinner and then head back to your place to spend some quality time together."

"Sounds good." I was disappointed he didn't want to stay tonight, but I knew he'd been playing catch up since he'd returned from his trip, so I didn't say anything.

"It looks like you have company," Cody commented when we approached my cabin.

"Ebenezer, what are you doing here?"

The large white cat simply rubbed his body through my legs. It still amazed me the way the cat managed to make his way from his home on Balthazar Pottage's island to Madrona Island whenever he felt the need to enlist my help.

"Is Balthazar okay?" I asked my furry friend after I let him into the house.

"Meow."

"You can take him back tomorrow to check out the situation," Cody suggested.

"I think I will. I'll call Tara to let her know I'll be late coming in."

Chapter 3

Tuesday, June 21

"Oh God, what happened?"

"Why would you think something happened?" Finn asked me early the next morning from his vantage point on my front stoop.

"Ebenezer showed up last night and you're here this morning. It can only mean one thing: something horrible has occurred."

Finn bowed his head. "I'm afraid you're right."

"Balthazar?"

"Alex."

"He's dead?" I realized my voice was all high and squeaky, but I felt like I was on the verge of complete hysteria.

"No. He's not dead. He's in jail."

I felt momentary relief. I mean, we'd all seen this coming. Maybe this would be the wake-up call he needed. "Does his arrest have to do with the party he probably had last night?"

"Indirectly. Daisy Farmer is dead and Alex is the number-one suspect."

All the blood rushed from my face. "What?"

"Maybe you should sit down." Finn took my arm and walked me back into my cabin. He sat me on the sofa before he continued. "Last night at approximately two a.m. the county office received a 911 call from an anonymous woman who said she was at a party and there was a dead woman in the pool. The county called and asked me to investigate. When I arrived at Alex's house I did indeed find a dead woman in the pool."

"She drowned?"

"She was stabbed and then dumped in the pool."

"And you think Alex did it?"

"By the time I arrived at the house everyone but Alex was gone. He was passed out on a lounge chair near the pool with blood all over his shirt."

"Oh God."

"The murder weapon, which turned out to be a knife from the set on the counter in the kitchen, was tossed into the shrubs nearby. It had Alex's fingerprints as well as Daisy's blood all over it."

The room started to spin as I listened to Finn speak. This couldn't be happening. Sure, Alex had changed, but I couldn't believe he'd changed so much that he was capable of killing someone in cold blood. There had to be another explanation.

"What did Alex say?"

"I haven't spoken to him yet. He was transported to the hospital, where he had his stomach pumped, and then he was taken into custody and is currently in a jail cell on San Juan Island."

"Does Balthazar know?"

"Not yet. My plan is to head over to San Juan Island to talk to Alex and then head out to Pottage's island to fill him in. I stopped here first because I wanted you to hear it from me and not through the rumor mill, which I'm sure will be going in full force before you even get to work."

"If you're going to talk to Balthazar I'm going with you." I stood up. "Just give me a couple of minutes to get dressed."

Finn decided it would be faster to take his boat than to wait for the ferry, so we headed to the marina where the boat was docked. I debated whether to take Ebenezer back to Balthazar, but it seemed clear to me that Ebenezer had come to Madrona Island to help me figure out what had occurred at Alex's house the previous evening. Though the last ferry to dock on Madrona did so at 8 p.m., which meant Ebenezer would have had to leave

Balthazar's island hours before the murder even took place.

Every now and then I try to figure out exactly what's going on with the cats Tansy sends me and how the whole thing works, but the reality was that I wouldn't know the answer to that question unless she decided to share what she knew, and so far she'd refused to explain much of anything. There were those who said Tansy, along with her roommate and business partner, Bella, were witches, but neither woman had been inclined to verify or deny their witchy status. Ultimately, I suppose it didn't really matter how it worked. In the end the only thing that was important was that it did, and the cats Tansy sent had always helped me solve whatever mystery I was working on.

"When we get to San Juan Island I'm going to have to go in to speak to Alex alone. You can watch through the two-way mirror. Is there anything specific you want me to ask him?" Finn asked. It seemed he already assumed I'd be working on this case, the way I had the others before it.

"I'm sure you're planning to find out what he remembers and get a list of everyone who was at the party last night. That's all that comes to mind off hand. Chances are the killer is someone who was there. I guess I'm most interested in the whereabouts of his friend Nick. He, Daisy, and Alex have been attached at the hip since Alex has been home. The fact that he wasn't with Alex when the body was discovered makes him the number-one suspect in my book."

When we arrived at the jail I was shown to a small room just off the interrogation room. I could see and hear what was being said inside, but neither Alex nor Finn could see or hear me.

"Do you know why you're here?" Finn asked Alex.

"Not really. I guess I must have passed out last night because I woke up a little while ago in the hospital. They wouldn't say what had happened, but after they discharged me they brought me here and said I had to wait for you. What's going on?"

"You don't remember?" Finn asked, although Alex had as much as just said he didn't. I supposed it was important to make sure Alex's testimony was in context to specific questions so there wasn't a misunderstanding along the way.

"No. I really don't remember. The whole thing is so odd."

"Why don't you tell me what you do remember and we'll take it from there?"

Alex fidgeted in his seat. I could see he was nervous. I couldn't really blame him. I'd be nervous too if I woke up in the hospital and then was taken to jail and I had no idea why and how I'd gotten there. Finn had given me a pad of paper and a pen and I began to take notes furiously as Alex continued to speak.

"I guess you know Nick and Daisy have been staying with me this summer. Daisy is a sweet girl, but Nick likes to party, so we've been doing a lot of entertaining. Last night Nick suggested we call some people and have them over, but I was tired, so I told him that I wanted to have an early night. Nick isn't the sort to want to sit around, so we compromised by agreeing to go out to dinner and *then* make it an early night. We went to Antonio's, which was when we saw you. Once Nick saw you were there he decided he didn't want to stay for dinner after all, so we went back to the house."

Alex ran his hand through his long hair. I remembered when I'd first discovered the reason he wore his hair long was to cover up a heart-shaped birthmark on his forehead.

"I went out to the pool for a swim and when I came back in Nick informed me that he'd called a few people to come over after all. I wasn't happy, but he promised he'd keep it small. And he did. At least in Nick terms."

"How many people are we talking about?" Finn asked.

Alex squinted as I imagined he did a head count. "Ten, including Nick, Daisy, and me."

"And who all was there?"

"A girl named Brittany Walters, who's been to several of our parties. She brought five guests, three guys and two girls. I don't know their names."

"And the tenth person?"

"A girl named Mallery Quinnley. Nick is sort of dating her, although he isn't exactly monogamous."

"Okay; what happened after everyone arrived?"

Alex took a deep breath. I could see he was confused.

"It's all so strange. I really didn't feel like partying, so I grabbed a soda and headed up to my room. I remember turning on the television while I drank the soda, but then everything went blank. The next thing I knew I woke up in the hospital."

"Had you done drugs that night?"

"No. I swear, I didn't even have a drink. I have no idea what happened."

Finn sat back and looked at Alex. I'd known Finn long enough to see he was trying to make up his mind about something. Probably whether he believed Alex's story.

"You were in the hospital to have your stomach pumped. You had a large quantity of a dangerous drug in your system. Enough to kill you, had you not been found. You have no recollection of how that drug came to be in your system?"

"No. I swear, I didn't take any drugs and the only thing I had to drink was the soda."

"Did anyone else have access to that soda?"

Alex hesitated. I wasn't sure if he didn't know or just didn't want to say.

"Please answer the question," Finn insisted.

"Daisy. She wanted me to grab some chips off a high shelf before I went upstairs, so I handed her my soda and asked her to hold it. But she wouldn't drug me. Ask her. She'll tell you it wasn't her."

Finn looked directly at Alex. "We can't ask Daisy whether she drugged your soda because she's dead."

"What?" Alex's face first reflected shock, quickly followed by grief. "She'd dead? How?"

"We believe, based on the evidence we've found, that you stabbed her and tossed her in the pool."

All the blood drained from Alex's face. "No," he insisted. "I wouldn't. I loved Daisy. I'd never hurt her."

"So she was your girlfriend?"

"No." Tears streamed down Alex's face. It appeared he was honestly grieving. "At least not yet."

"Can you explain that?"

Alex hung his head and wept. Finn waited. After a couple of minutes he handed Alex a tissue. Alex dried his eyes. "I met Daisy in college," he began, looking at Finn. "She was beautiful, with a sunny smile and an equally sunny disposition. I fell for her the first time I saw her, but she didn't know me from a knot in the door. I knew she was out of my league. She was rich and beautiful and could have pretty much any guy she wanted. Still, I worshiped her from afar even though I knew I didn't have a chance."

"So what changed?"

"I met Nick, who told me that if I wanted to have a shot with Daisy I had to change my lifestyle. He said she only went for rich guys with fast cars and designer clothes. I'd been living simply, but I did have the money Balthazar sent me for school expenses. I had a scholarship, so I didn't really need it for school; it had just been sitting in my savings account. I decided to use it to buy a brand-new car and a whole new wardrobe. Nick convinced me that even with the expensive car Daisy was never going to notice me if I continued to spend my nights studying and volunteering at the local homeless shelter. He said if I wanted her, I had to attend all the right parties and know all the right people. He offered to introduce me around and I let him. Eventually, Daisy did notice me and we became friends."

"How did Nick know Daisy in the first place?"

"She's his sister. Does Nick know what happened to Daisy?"

"Nick wasn't there when we arrived last night, and as far as I know, he hasn't been located yet. So, you said you and Daisy were only friends?"

"Yes. I hoped for more, and I think our time together this summer was moving me closer to that becoming a reality, but as of yesterday we were still just friends."

"Do you have any idea why anyone would want her dead?"

"No. She's just a sweet, simple girl."

She didn't sound sweet and simple to me. In fact, both Daisy and her brother sounded like users who'd been living all summer on Alex's dime.

"I didn't kill her," Alex insisted.

"There was blood on your shirt and your fingerprints are all over the murder weapon."

"They are?" Alex put his hand to his mouth. I was sure he was going to vomit, but he managed to get his body under control after Finn handed him a glass of water.

"I don't know what happened, but I intend to find out," Finn assured him. "In the meantime, Alex Turner, you are under arrest for the murder of Daisy Farmer. You have the right to remain silent. Anything you say can be used against you...."

I watched as Alex sat like a statue while Finn read him his rights. Alex had been unconscious when they'd found him at his home, so this was the first opportunity for anyone to do it. I wondered about the legality of him being held while he waited for Finn, but Finn explained to me later that Alex was being held on a drug charge for the illegal narcotic found in his system, not murder, until Finn got there.

"What do you think?" I asked Finn as we left the jail and headed toward Balthazar's island.

"I don't know what to think. The guy seemed to be telling the truth. It seems possible someone else killed Daisy and is framing Alex. I just have to figure out who."

"We have the list from the party. Well, we don't know the names of Brittany Walter's friends, but I'm sure she'll tell us if we ask her."

"Which I plan to do after we speak to Pottage."

"He's going to take this hard."

"Yeah." Finn sighed. "I'm sure he will. Still, it's best he hears it from us and not someone else. Alex is going to need an attorney. A good one. I'm sure Pottage knows a number of them."

As predicted, Balthazar was devastated when he heard the news. He blamed himself for giving Alex too much money too soon. He should have waited to begin turning over assets until he was able to work with Alex so he would know how to handle wealth. He would hire the best attorney money could buy to represent Alex and made me promise to get to the bottom of the whole thing, whatever it took. I of course promised him I'd do my best. Balthazar decided Ebenezer should stay with me until the case was solved. He wanted to be near his son, so he planned to rent something on San Juan Island, and Finn and I dropped him off on our way back to Madrona.

Chapter 4

Somewhere along the way, in the midst of solving a string of local murders, I'd gathered a sleuthing gang. There were times when certain members were more involved than others, but when there was a mystery that needed to be solved, you could bet that at some point I'd get together with Cody, Tara, Siobhan, Finn, and Danny to build theories and test hypotheses.

Cody had brought pizza to share, Danny beer, and, as she had since she'd first introduced the concept, Siobhan took charge of the murder board.

Finn and I shared what we'd learned earlier in the day and Danny and Cody asked questions and offered insights as we nibbled and drank.

Siobhan started off by listing the main players on the whiteboard: Alex, Nick, and Daisy. "Daisy is the victim, Alex is in jail although he claims he's innocent, and Nick is missing," Siobhan began.

"He still hasn't turned up?" I asked Finn.

"Not so far. I have an all-points bulletin out for him, but so far he hasn't shown up on the ferry or in any of his usual local hangouts. If he was trying to disappear I'm going to assume he left the island by private boat."

"He most likely didn't kill his own sister," Tara offered.

"Probably not," Finn agreed, "although most murders *are* carried out by someone close to the victim. Given the fact that he's disappeared, he remains a strong suspect."

"Okay; who else?" Siobhan asked.

"Mallery Quinnley," Finn answered. "I interviewed her after we returned to the island. She said she's been sort of dating Nick, although they weren't exclusive, and he called her last night and wanted her to come over. She was tired and was about to decline, but then she decided to stop by for a few minutes. She said she had one drink and left shortly after Alex went up to his room. She indicated that she hadn't seen or spoken to Nick, or anyone else who was at the party, since then."

"Do we believe her?" Siobhan asked.

Finn shrugged. "She didn't do or say anything that would suggest she was lying."

"Okay, who's next?" Siobhan stood with her marker poised to write.

"Brittany Walters came to the party and brought five guests: Dirk Nesbeth, Connor Littleman, Eric Cassidy, Val Corning, and Stephanie Young. I haven't been able to get hold of Brittany, but when I spoke to Mallery she remembered the names of her guests. Mallery said that as far as she knew, none of them had been to previous parties at Alex's place, and she didn't know why Brittany brought those specific individuals."

Siobhan wrote down all the names. "And what do we know about each?"

"I know Val wanted to go to one of Alex's parties something awful," I contributed. "I ran into her in town yesterday and she told me she'd do just about anything to be able to attend. She even asked me to talk to Alex to see if I could get her an invite. I don't know how she got from hopeless to invited in the course of a few hours, but you can bet she isn't going to have shown up late, gotten tired, and left early like Mallery. I'll bet once she was invited she was going to stay until they kicked her out. Oh, and she had a thing for Nick. I'm betting if Mallery left Nick and Val might have hooked up."

"Have you had a chance to speak to Val?" Siobhan asked Finn.

"Not yet. I need to be on San Juan Island tomorrow to testify in the trial of a man I arrested a while back, so they're going to assign someone else to cover Madrona Island for a few days. I'd prefer that none of you shares information with my replacement. We can continue to get together in the evenings if we need to. I'm sure whoever they send will be a great cop, but I'm pretty sure the county would frown on my working with you all the way I do."

"Not a problem," Siobhan assured Finn. "What else do you have?"

"Dirk Nesbeth and Connor Littleman went to high school here," I volunteered. "They were a year or two behind me so I don't know either well, but I do know they're partiers. I don't know Eric Cassidy or Stephanie Young."

"Stephanie has been in the bookstore a few times," Tara said. "I think she moved to Madrona Island a few years ago. She works as a bartender over at Harding Pizza. I'm not surprised she snagged an invite to the party. She's really pretty and superoutgoing. I really doubt she's a killer, but she might have seen something."

We continued to discuss the various suspects a while longer, but none of us really had any insight into who might have killed Daisy. Finn pointed out that at this point we were totally lacking a motive, but we all thought one would probably present itself as the investigation progressed.

I was happy when Cody remained behind after the others left. I opened a bottle of wine, which we took out onto the deck overlooking the ocean. The sky had grown dark while we'd been inside, but the evening was warm, perfect for simply relaxing. The cats followed us out onto the deck. Max burned up some of his excess energy by running around on the beach, while Ebenezer crawled into my lap and began to purr.

"I'm afraid this one might be tough," I said to Cody.

"They're all tough."

"Maybe, but this time I feel this huge urgency to solve the crime and solve it fast. I just can't believe Alex is guilty of killing Daisy and I hate to think of him sitting in jail with only his thoughts for company. Even if he didn't kill the woman I'm sure he feels guilty for the part he played in the setup of the situation."

"What do you mean?"

"If he hadn't been pursuing her he wouldn't have invited her and her brother to the island for the summer, and if she hadn't been on the island she wouldn't have ended up dead."

"Actually, we don't know that," Cody said.

"You think someone other than the people at the party could have killed her?"

"I think it's possible. Sure, the people at the party make logical suspects, but it isn't as if Alex's house is inaccessible. Anyone could have come by and killed Daisy. It could have been someone who knows her from college or her regular life, or it could even have been a random act by someone bent on robbing a bunch of rich kids."

I frowned. "Why didn't you bring that up before?"

Cody shrugged. "I guess I figured Finn already considered it. He's a cop. Yeah, he seems to be focusing on the partygoers, but I can promise you he's looking at other angles as well."

Cody had a point. Without any idea of a motive, we really had no idea who might have killed Daisy.

"I guess all we can do is start with the list we have and eliminate each suspect or not and then move on from there."

"That seems like the best plan." Cody nodded. "It might not hurt to look into Nick and Daisy and their past as well. I'm not sure why, but I have a feeling the killer could very well turn out to be someone from Daisy's past."

"That's a good idea. Of course if the killer turns out to be someone other than one of the party guests, we're going to have a really hard time tracking them down."

"I'm sure someone saw something. Once we have a chance to interview everyone we should have a better picture of what happened. Do you want another glass of wine?"

"Please." I waited while Cody poured us both a second glass. It seemed as if he planned to stay over, so I wanted to change the subject to something a bit more upbeat. The moon was glistening on the water and the night was warm and still. We'd done what we could for today; it was time to relax and enjoy the rest of the evening. "Did I tell you that Maggie got a call from Haley yesterday, letting her know that her dad was fine with her coming here for the rest of the summer?"

"No. That's great. I know Maggie misses her."

Haley was a thirteen-year-old girl I'd first met the previous summer when she'd come to stay with her aunt during her mother's illness. After her mother died, the aunt went home but Haley stayed on with Maggie, helping with the cats until it was time for school to start in the fall.

"Maggie is superexcited to have her and I bet Siobhan is going to love her. Besides, she's a big help with the cats, and Maggie and I are both so busy at our shops during the summer."

"You know," Cody said after I'd finished speaking, "you should see if Haley's interested in joining that adopt-a-grandparent program I wrote an article about a few weeks ago."

The program was for kids between the ages of thirteen and seventeen who each adopted a senior citizen in their community to help with light chores and provide company. All the seniors were prescreened so as to weed out anyone with a criminal record, and the kids visited the seniors in pairs to ensure their safety. It was of great help to the elderly who were housebound, and I was certain Haley would enjoy participating in such an awesome group.

"That's a great idea. I'll suggest it to Maggie. I brought it up to Cassie, but I'm afraid my little sister is more of an angsty teen than a helpful one."

"This whole thing with your mom has to be hard on her. It's hard on all of you, but when your mom moves away to live with Reginald it's going to disrupt Cassie's whole world."

"Siobhan seems to have managed to convince Mom to let Cassie live with her and Maggie, but it's still going to be a difficult transition. Aiden has even mentioned giving up fishing in order to stay at home with Cassie until she turns eighteen, but I don't think that would be the best solution. Aiden loves fishing. It's in his blood. I'm afraid if he gave it up he'd just turn into a moody old man like my dad did right before he died."

"It's hard to give up what you love."

"I realize that change is inevitable, but it seems like the best kinds are the ones you're ready for," I commented. "Anything that's thrust upon you can be hard to deal with and I don't think Aiden is quite ready to settle down and stay in one place year-round. On the other hand, Cassie will be eighteen in two years, so it isn't as if Aiden would have to give up the lifestyle that suits him best permanently."

"Maybe Siobhan should just move into your mother's house with Cassie," Cody suggested.

"That's actually not a bad idea. I'll suggest it to Siobhan. She seems to be committed to staying on the island now, while she's mayor, so moving home to take care of Cassie might actually work out for everyone. Of course even if Cassie doesn't have to move, having Mom gone will be a big change for her."

"Speaking of change, I was wondering if you'd be willing to help me redecorate my apartment."

"Redecorate? I thought you liked what you'd done with the place."

"I did. At first. But all I really did was clean out my storage shed and set things around. Now that I've lived in the space for a while I've come to realize that a lot of the things from my old life don't really go with certain aspects of my new one. In fact, a lot of the things I've been hanging on to I've only kept because I really couldn't see getting rid of them."

"Hey, if you want to redecorate I'm happy to help, but you really should ask Siobhan. She has more talent in that area than I do."

"I don't care about talent; I care about creating a space where you feel comfortable. It occurred to me that we've never once spent the night at my place. I come here or we sleep in our separate homes. I hope if we have the option of staying at either place we might actually be able to spend more time together."

"What about Mr. Parsons? Won't he mind if Max and I stay over?"

Cody wound his fingers through mine. "First of all, I have my own apartment on the third floor of his house and he never leaves the first floor, so I don't think we'll bother him, and secondly, I already asked him if he minded and he said he didn't in the least."

"Well, okay then. I'm open to the idea when I don't have a cat in residence and a murder to solve. In the meantime, would you like to stay here tonight?"

Cody pulled a toothbrush out of his pocket. "I was planning on it and came prepared."

"That's all you brought?"

"That's all I'll need."

Chapter 5

Wednesday, June 22

The first ferry of the day was just pulling into the dock when I dropped Cody off at the newspaper and settled the four cats I'd brought to feature that day into the cat lounge. When Tara and I used to dream about Coffee Cat Books before it was a reality, we both agreed that finding a way to incorporate the cats so as to provide a platform to aide in the adoption goals of Harthaven Cat Sanctuary was a must.

The sanctuary was really the brainchild of my Aunt Maggie, who'd wanted to rescue and protect the feral cats on the island when our former mayor pushed through a law allowing residents to remove any cats on their property by any means necessary. The aforementioned mayor had since passed on, so the cats weren't in as much danger as they previously had been, but the sanctuary had caught on and difficult-to-adopt cats from all over the state were now making their way to our facility.

The younger cats and kittens were altered, socialized, and rehomed, while the older cats we deemed unadoptable were comfortably housed and allowed to live out their lives with us.

Today I had an appointment with a woman from Orcas Island who was interested in a young, box-trained cat for her daughter. I'd spoken to the woman on the phone and her household situation seemed perfect for one of our cats, but when I met her four-year-old daughter, Lilli Reid, an adorable pixie with brown hair and curious eyes, I knew the ten-month-old, longhaired tabby she'd bonded with the moment she laid eyes on her would be a perfect match.

Mrs. Reid's friend, Mrs. Lansing, a middle-aged woman who loved to crochet and read and, I knew, would provide a comfortable lap for one of my kitties, sat with the remaining three felines while Lilli's mother and I filled out the necessary paperwork required for our adoptions.

"I think what you're doing here is just wonderful," Mrs. Reid commented. "I love how you've integrated the cats into the bookstore. It's always been a dream of mine to own a bookstore, but I would never had thought to include the cats."

"I love all three of the remaining cats," Mrs. Lansing said, "but I think I'm going to have to choose the small black one. She has a look of mystery in her bright green eyes."

I handed Mrs. Lansing her own application to fill out and chatted with both women until I noticed Val Corning coming into the bookstore and stopping to chat with Tara.

"If you'll excuse me, there's someone I need to speak to in the other room. Stay and visit with the cats for as long as you like. And when you're finished with the paperwork just let me know."

I could see Tara and Destiny Paulson, our assistant, were swamped with the crowd from the ferry and this probably wasn't the best time to have a conversation about Daisy's murder with Val. I hoped she'd provide us with some additional information, so the fact that she'd basically come to me was too good an opportunity to ignore.

"Oh, good, you're here," Val said when I came into the bookstore side of the building. "I didn't see you at first, so I was afraid you weren't in today."

"I take it you want to talk about what happened at Alex's place?"

Val looked around nervously, then leaned in close and lowered her voice. "I need to tell someone what I know."

"The crowd from the ferry should thin out in about a half hour. Can you meet me back here then? I'd talk to you now, but we wouldn't have much privacy."

Val looked at her watch. "Yeah, okay. This is too important to be overheard. I'll be back in thirty minutes."

I had the sense that Val was interested in more than a good gossip. She seemed genuinely scared. I probably should have taken the time to talk with her immediately, but it had been more than a day since the murder; another half hour shouldn't matter in the least.

Unfortunately, a half hour made all the difference in the world. After Val left Coffee Cat Books she was mugged, or at least that was the determination that was made by Finn's replacement. If you ask me, the fact that she was hit over the head and was now in the hospital on San Juan Island had a lot more to do with what she'd been about to tell me than it did with the twenty-three dollars and seventy-two cents she told the deputy was in her wallet.

I texted Finn and filled him in on what had occurred. I hoped he'd be able to talk to Val to find out what it was she'd been intent on sharing with me. Finn would be tied up for the rest of the afternoon, but maybe he'd have time to stop by the hospital to see her when court recessed for the day.

"I hope Val's going to be okay," Destiny said as she fed her son James, who was now six months old. Most of the time he stayed with a babysitter while Destiny worked, but the sitter was sick and we'd really needed Destiny's help this week, so we'd set up a crib in the back and a play area near the coffee counter.

"Yeah, me too. I sort of feel responsible for what happened."

"You couldn't have known," Destiny insisted.

"Yeah, but Val came in wanting to talk to me and I asked her to come back. The borrowed deputy seemed to think it was a random robbery, but I feel certain the attacker was more concerned about silencing Val than stealing her purse."

"Have you heard back from Finn?" Tara asked.

I shook my head. "I didn't actually speak to him. I texted him, but he was still in court, so he just texted back that he'd look into it when he was free."

I glanced at the clock. It was already six and time to close. Cody and I normally had choir practice on Wednesdays, but the church was being used for a wedding that evening so we'd postponed practice to the following evening.

"I should get going." Destiny stood up. "I'm supposed to go to my mom's for dinner tonight and she hates it when I'm late. I input the new inventory into the computer this afternoon. Part of it has been shelved and I'll finish up the rest when I come in tomorrow."

"Thanks, Destiny," Tara said. "I appreciate all the extra hours you've worked."

"I'm happy to help out, but I do hope we can find some extra help before July rolls around. I'm not sure the three of us will be able to keep up."

"Cait and I have interviews lined up for tomorrow morning," Tara confirmed.

Destiny left, turning off the "open" sign on her way out, and I began straightening the shelves while Tara reconciled the cash register. I really loved the little business Tara and I had built, but I had to agree with Destiny that we needed help and needed it fast. As long as no one came in looking for a cat at the same time the crowd from the ferry was in the store ordering drinks and buying books we were generally okay, but on days like today, when the cat adoption business had been brisk, the lines at the checkout register tended to dissuade window shoppers from coming in.

"I noticed Cassie was in earlier," Tara commented.

"Yeah. She'd had a fight with Mom and wanted to vent."

"Are they fighting a lot?"

"Every day. This whole wedding thing has left Cassie unbalanced. She seems depressed, which worries me."

"Maybe you should talk to her about coming to work for us this summer. She's helped out before, and maybe it would be a good thing if she had time away from your mother."

"I'll ask her about it again. I mentioned it a month or so ago, before school was out, but at the time she wanted to get a job that would allow her to hang out with her friends. I know she applied at the marina as well as a couple of fast-food joints, but for some reason nothing has seemed to work out. For one thing, Mom is dead set against her working on

Sundays, and a lot of the places where she put in applications require them."

"Yeah, the Sunday thing is tough. I know we've tossed around the idea of opening on Sundays during the summer. I'm sure it would help our cash flow a lot. Still, we do need time to spend with family, and we don't have enough help to cover the shifts and still take time off."

"Maybe by next summer we'll be able to afford to hire a manager to oversee things when neither one of us is here," I said.

"That's what I'm hoping for as well." Tara nodded toward the front door. "Looks like you have company."

"What is he doing here?" I went over to the door, unlocked it, and let Ebenezer in.

"He was probably tired of waiting for you to get off." Tara laughed. "He really isn't the sort to want to sit around. At least he waited until we were closed this time."

When Ebenezer had helped me solve the case of the missing son last December he'd come by the bookstore several times, each one when we were open.

"If you have some clue you want to show me it will need to be fast," I informed the cat. "Cody's coming over at seven and I'm hoping Finn will come over with news too."

"Meow." Ebenezer jumped up onto the counter and lay down next to where Tara was counting the money.

"Yes, Tara is invited as well," I added. I looked at her. "If you want to."

"I'd love to come over and hang out if everyone else is, but I don't want to be a third wheel if it turns out it's going to be just you and Cody."

"I'll text you after I hear from Finn."

"Why don't you go ahead and go with Ebenezer? I'll finish locking up and doing the day-end chores," Tara offered.

I had my car, but Ebenezer seemed to want to walk, so I followed him down Main Street. With the arrival of the long days of summer most of the retail outlets stayed open until at least eight o'clock, but Tara and I had decided that if we were going to maintain our sanity during our busiest months a workday that spanned the eight hours between ten and six was plenty. The truth of the matter was, even with eight hours of operation, Tara almost always came in by eight and we usually stayed in the store until past seven.

Ebenezer led me down the street to a place where there was a small pathway between two buildings that led to the alleyway behind the shops. The opening was narrow but quite passable for a cat and a very petite woman. He darted into the opening, stopping to look back at me when I didn't follow immediately.

"If you're heading to the alley let's go the long way around. That little pathway is covered with cobwebs. I'm meeting Cody in less than an hour. I don't want cobwebs in my hair."

Ebenezer meowed but refused to budge. I was about to walk away and continue on down to the street that linked Main with the alley when I noticed the sun reflecting off an object just beyond where Ebenezer was waiting.

"All right," I mumbled, "but that shiny thing had better be a clue or a gold coin because I'm going to be pretty mad if I end up with cobwebs in my hair only to find an empty soda can."

As it turned out, the object Ebenezer led me to wasn't a soda can but a phone. Based on the cat displayed on the lock screen, the phone belonged to none other than Val Corning.

It turned out that Finn had been able to speak to Val briefly, but unfortunately she wasn't talking. She'd told Finn her injury left her feeling confused and light-headed and she couldn't remember what it was she'd wanted to speak to me about or who had attacked her. Finn had the feeling she was lying. Val was able to provide the passcode to her phone, however, and there were a few things contained on it that I felt led to a significant clue.

Finn told me that he'd been asked to dinner by his boss, the sheriff, so it was going to be late before he made it back to the island. He suggested we go ahead and meet to talk things through and he'd join us later if he had the opportunity. Cody was already at my place and Tara had still been at the bookstore when I returned there, so I called Siobhan and Danny and invited them to join us. As had become custom for these impromptu gatherings, someone brought food and someone else brought beer.

"Man, how much do I love this weather?" Danny sighed as we gathered around the picnic table on my deck, which overlooked the water. "Every single one of my whale-watch tours is booked for the next month. I'm even thinking about adding an additional tour in the early evening. Sort of a pre-sunset cruise. All the sunset cruises are booked solid, but there's a window of time between the afternoon and the sunset cruises."

"You mean the window you now use to eat something and work on the boat if it needs it?" Tara commented.

"Yeah, I know it'll be tight, but it was a weak winter income wise and I have a lot of maintenance and repairs to do to the boat that I've been putting off. The extra income would be welcome."

I noticed several whales in the distance. It looked like a small pod enjoying the last rays of sun. There were at least four whale-watch boats nearby and I had to wonder why Danny was sitting with us and not out on the water if the tours were as packed as he'd indicated, so I asked him.

"I'd already told a friend of mine he could use the boat to take his family out for his parents' wedding anniversary. You remember Toby Green?"

"Yeah, I remember Toby. How's he doing?"

"Good. He's thinking about moving back to the island and opening up a restaurant."

I noticed the interest on Tara's face. She'd had a thing for Toby when we were in high school. They'd never dated, and I wasn't sure Toby even knew how she'd felt, but it hadn't really mattered because he'd moved away from the island shortly after graduation.

"What sort of a restaurant?" I wondered.

"Steaks and burgers. He has his eye on one of the abandoned houses on the north shore. He thinks people will be willing to make the drive to dine in a house converted into a restaurant overlooking the water."

"I think he might be right," Tara contributed. "I've dined in other restaurants that are really just converted houses and they were charming. It allows you to create microenvironments in the various rooms. The last house I dined in had theme rooms that were really charming. I hope it works out for him."

"Just be sure he gets the proper paperwork," Siobhan coached in her mayor voice. "The island council is cracking down on businesses operating without permits."

"What did you find on the phone?" Cody asked. He was right; it was time to get back on track.

"Two things so far that seem relevant," I answered. "The first is Val's call history. I wanted to see if she was the one who called in the 911 the night Daisy was killed, but she wasn't. At least not from this phone."

"Seems like the detective investigating the case would already know from which phone that call originated," Cody pointed out. "I bet it was the landline at the house. If it was a cell I'm sure the sheriff's office would have acted on that and Finn would know about it.'

"True. I hadn't thought of that," I had to admit. "I was also curious as to how she came to be at the party, so I looked for a call we could trace back to either Nick, who organized the party, or Brittany, who she came with, but after verifying the numbers I found I didn't find calls to or from either of them."

"Maybe they were together when Brittany got the call and she invited Val verbally," Tara suggested.

"That's my guess as well."

"And the other thing?" Siobhan asked. "You said there were two things."

I pulled up a photo from the gallery. The last photo Val had taken, as a matter of fact. It was dark, but a flash had been used, so it was pretty easy to make out the details in the photo: Daisy floating facedown in the pool and Alex passed out in a nearby lawn chair.

"What do you notice?" I asked as I passed the phone around.

"No blood," Cody commented.

"Cody's right," Siobhan seconded. "Finn said Alex had blood on his shirt, but in this photo Daisy is clearly dead but Alex's shirt is clean."

"Which means that someone changed his shirt and dressed him in the bloody one at some point after Daisy was already dead," I pointed out.

"Or someone might have sprayed blood on the shirt he was wearing after this photo was taken," Siobhan added.

"This proves Alex was set up," Tara stated.

"It proves it to me," I agreed. "I forwarded a copy of the photo to Finn and he thinks he can get Alex out of jail as early as tonight."

"Good work, Ebenezer." Tara picked up the large cat and scratched him under the chin.

"The question is," Danny said, "if Alex didn't kill Daisy, who did?"

"I don't know," I admitted. "And after what happened to Val I'm concerned for both her and Alex's safety. Finn said Val might have died if the attacker hadn't been interrupted by a group of tourists, who claim to have no idea what the attacker looked like, by the way. And Alex would have died from the overdose if whoever called 911 hadn't done it when they did. Whoever killed Daisy doesn't seem reluctant to kill again if need be."

Chapter 6

Thursday, June 23

The newspaper with the photo of Ariel had been published on Wednesday and I hoped Ariel and Rosalyn would be united by now, but when I called her dad that morning he informed me that while there had been a lot of calls from people claiming to have seen Ariel, so far no one had been able to catch her. We both hoped the sightings were real; if they were at least we'd know she was still alive.

I left for Coffee Cat Books a little early. I wanted to drive around Pelican Bay to see if I could spot the dog. Most stray animals found their way to the alley behind Main, where the dumpsters for all the local businesses were stored. While driving slowly through the alley didn't yield any results, it did give me the idea to distribute Ariel's photo to the local garbage collectors as well as to the local postal carriers. Employees from both made the rounds around town on a regular basis.

When it became clear I wasn't going to find Ariel on that particular morning I headed for the bookstore and the interviews we'd planned.

"And have you had experience working as a barista?" I asked the second woman Tara and I had interviewed that morning. We'd set up the interviews so we could complete them before the store opened at ten, so each person had only fifteen minutes to wow us.

"No, not really," Brenda DuBois answered. Brenda was a local woman with a sunny personality that shone through as noticeably as her big hair and equally ample bosom. "But I'm great with people and I know how to engage the interest of anyone who walks through that door."

"It says here you worked at the Dairy Queen in Seattle," Tara said.

"I was known for making the best Blizzards in town. And I always have a joke to share with the customers. I can only work until school starts back up in the fall because I have five children who participate in various sports and afterschool events, but I sure would like an excuse to get out of the house during the summer when they're all home."

I smiled. Five kids. Yikes; I'd want to get out of the house too.

"Okay, well, thank you for your time," Tara wrapped up. "We have several other applicants to interview, but we'll be in touch one way or the other by the end of the week."

"Five kids. The poor thing," I said after she left.

"Yeah, I can see she has a legitimate reason for wanting a summer job, but I think we need someone with more experience. Who's next?"

"Kathy Livermore."

"Oh, I know her." Tara smiled. "She's one of our best customers."

"The name doesn't ring a bell," I admitted.

"That's because we call her the dog lady."

"Oh, her name is Kathy. She's great, and she knows everything there is about pretty much every book that comes out. I can't decide which she loves more, books or dogs, but are we sure she wants to work in a cat lounge? She does seem to prefer dogs."

"I guess we'll need to get a feel for that. The last two candidates are Ruth

Hallmark and Roni Waverly. Ruth has a lot of experience in retail, especially gifts and cards, which we've decided to expand into a lot more than we have in the past, but Roni actually has the most experience. She's worked as a barista and has spent quite a bit of time in retail. If I had to hire off the applications alone I'd say she'll probably end up being the one we choose, but let's talk to the other two just in case. Maybe they'll want to help with some of the events we have planned or run one of our book clubs."

Luckily for us, Kathy was very interested in running one of our book clubs and Ruth was eager to help with our booth sales at the community events coming up over the summer. Roni, who was a wiz behind the coffee bar, was as knowledgeable as she appeared on paper and was agreeable to all our terms, including hours and pay. The crowds we'd been experiencing already were only the tip of the iceberg, so it was good we'd found someone so perfect on our first round of interviews.

"I'm meeting Cody for a late breakfast/early lunch," I informed Tara. "Do you want me to bring you something?"

"A sandwich would be great. Turkey on whole wheat."

"I shouldn't be long," I promised, "and Destiny should be back from her doctor's appointment any minute."

I'd arranged to meet Cody at the newspaper because I wasn't sure exactly when I'd be done with the interviews. He was on the phone when I arrived and waved at me when I walked in through the front door. Cody had done a great job rejuvenating the paper after he'd bought it the previous summer. He'd taken a small press with community appeal and turned it into a small press with both a local and state following via the internet presence he'd established.

"I do think that will make an interesting article. I'll see what I can do," Cody said to whoever was on the other end of the line. "I'll try to make it."

"Get a lead on a story?" I asked as soon as he hung up.

"Mrs. Pitmore's cat is having kittens. She figured that because it had won a cat show last spring, the fact that the little darling was reproducing was newsworthy. My first instinct was to remind her that I'm trying to make sure the *Madrona Island News* is a serious newspaper that covers newsworthy items of greater importance than spelling bees and baby cats, but then I remembered that it's spelling bees and baby animals that built this paper in the first place."

"So you're going to do an article on her kittens?"

"Yes. And a few photos won't hurt."

"Any news on Ariel?" I asked.

"I've had a ton of phone calls, most legit but others seeming more like people fishing for additional information about the reward we offered. So far no one has managed to catch up with the dog. Those who remember seeing her before seeing the article in the paper didn't realize the dog was lost and those who saw her after reading the article and tried to catch her say she ran off as soon as she was approached."

"She's probably scared. First the trip to the island, then being on her own in a strange place. Poor thing."

Cody squeezed my hand. "Don't worry, we'll find her. What do you want to eat?"

"I told Tara I wouldn't be long, so let's just go down to the Driftwood."

The Driftwood Café was just a few doors down from the paper and served both breakfast and lunch at this time of day. It was a popular joint for locals and visitors alike, so Cody and I took seats at the counter rather than waiting for a table. I ordered a spicy scramble and Cody chose a tuna melt with fries.

"Did you ever hear from Finn?" Cody asked. He'd never made it by the previous evening.

"He texted to say he had court again today and probably tomorrow but hadn't managed to get much out of Val other than what we already knew. She's obviously terrified of someone, so he's going to put her into protective custody when she gets out of the hospital. He's hoping if she feels safe she'll be willing to talk."

"And Alex?"

"Still in jail. The district attorney claims the photo could have been altered to make it look as though there's no blood on the shirt. Finn thinks he's grasping, but right now he's refusing to drop the charges. If Val actually remembers seeing Alex and can verify that Daisy was already dead before the blood somehow made its way onto his shirt, the DA will have no choice but to let him go."

"Chances are it's the guilty party who hit Val and probably threatened to do a whole lot more if she talked. I don't really blame her for being scared."

"Yeah. Me neither."

"Do we know when she's being released from the hospital?"

"Finn thinks sometime today. We can get an update this evening. We have choir, but Finn said he's fine with coming by after. He indicated that he has a few things he wants to discuss that he wasn't comfortable talking about over the phone. Siobhan plans to come by as well, so we should probably pick up some food."

"We'll let the parents know tonight will be a short rehearsal when they drop their kids off," Cody said. "I'd cancel altogether, but we have that new song premiering on Sunday and half of the kids can't seem to remember the lyrics."

"We could wait until a later date to premier it," I suggested.

"We could, but Trish has the solo and her grandparents are going to be in town, so I promised her we'd do it this week."

"That was nice of you."

"I'm a nice guy."

When I returned to the bookstore after lunch I found Siobhan chatting with Tara.

"Oh good, you're back," Siobhan, who was stylishly dressed in a yellow dress with matching heels, commented.

"Were you looking for me?"

"Sort of. I came by to talk to both you and Tara about the Fourth of July, which, as you know, is just around the corner. We're hoping the four-day event we have planned will attract a lot of day visitors from the mainland, and it's my job as mayor to make sure everything is in place."

"Tara and I plan to enter a Coffee Cat Books float in the parade and we've reserved a booth for the street fair on Saturday," I told my sister.

"I have you down for both, but I was also hoping I could count on you to help with the pancake breakfast on Saturday and the street dance Friday evening."

"I'm game, as long as Tara has enough help at the store."

"I'll work it out," Tara confirmed.

"I was hoping both of you would be willing to help with the community picnic on Sunday because the bookstore is closed. I've organized a softball game and a kiddie carnival that afternoon, and of course we'll have the BBQ, which I hope will raise a lot of money for town projects."

Tara and I said we were willing to do whatever Siobhan needed. I noticed she seemed overly amped up about the events, which were held every year, but I supposed she was anxious for everything to go off without a hitch because this was the first we'd be having it since she'd been mayor.

"I also wanted to let you guys know that I spoke to Connor Littleman this morning." Connor had been one of the guests at the party at which Daisy had died. "He's working in construction now and he just happened to come with his boss to a meeting I had this morning with the developer who wants to build that new professional building. I pulled him aside after the meeting and asked him about the party."

"And...?"

"And he said Daisy was very much alive when he left. I asked him what time that was and who was still there, and he said it was around midnight and that there were six people other than Nick, Alex, and Daisy still at the house."

"Brittany Walters, Val Corning, Stephanie Young, Dirk Nesbeth, Eric Cassidy, and who else?" I asked. "Mallery said she left early, right after Alex went upstairs."

"Connor said Dirk went home before he did but that two men who were quite a bit older than the rest showed up at around eleven. He didn't know their names, but he thought Nick wasn't happy to see them. In fact, it was his opinion that Nick didn't know the men were even on the island."

"Did Connor give you a description of them?"

"Not really. He admitted to being drunk by the time they arrived. His general impression was that they both were fairly tall—at least six feet—and both had dark hair."

"Well, if we believe Connor we can cross him and Dirk off the suspect list because Daisy was alive when they left and add the two late arrivals. I'll just refer to them as Unknown One and Unknown Two for the time being."

"I asked Connor how it was he managed to get the invite to the party and he said he was hanging out at O'Malley's when Brittany got a call from Nick. She asked everyone who happened to be sitting at the bar if they wanted to go to a party and Connor, Dirk, Eric, Val, and Stephanie all jumped at the chance."

"So the guests she brought were random, not planned," I mused. I wondered if that was an important factor. It would seem the fact that the people were spontaneously chosen eliminated the possibility that any of the five last-minute guests came to the party with the intention of killing Daisy and framing Alex. Still, it seemed it would be worthwhile to have a chat with all of them.

"It looks like the ferry is almost here," Tara observed.

"I should get going anyway," Siobhan said.

"Are you going to come by after choir like we discussed?" I asked.

"I'll be there," Siobhan confirmed.

Tara decline. "I have a date."

"Really? Someone new?"

"Actually, someone old."

"Old?"

Tara just winked and walked away. Great, now I'd probably spend the rest of the day trying to figure out who Tara's mysterious date was.

Chapter 7

After work I stopped off at my cabin to change my clothes and let Max out and the first thing I noticed was that Ebenezer was nowhere in sight. I told myself not to worry, that the cat seemed to come and go on his own timetable, but still, I was concerned. Balthazar was counting on me to take care of him while he was on San Juan Island trying to help Alex, and I'd become really fond of the cat and hated to think something might have happened to him.

When he still hadn't returned by the time I had to leave for choir I decided to leave a window open so he could get in while I was away. I didn't even stop to consider how he'd gotten out in the first place; all the windows that didn't have screens had been locked.

As soon as I arrived at the church I was relieved to see Ebenezer sitting on the stoop in front of the church, chatting with Father Kilian. At least it looked like they were chatting. Father Kilian was clearly speaking and it looked as though Ebenezer was listening intently.

"There you are, you silly cat. I was worried about you."

"It seems Ebenezer wishes to attend choir practice with you this evening," Father Kilian informed me. "I tried to tell him that cats weren't allowed inside the church building, but he was quite insistent, so I decided to make an exception this one time."

"Meow," Ebenezer said before trotting in through the open door and down the hall toward the choir room.

"Ebenezer told you he wanted to go to choir practice?"

"In his own way. He's a very smart cat."

"Yeah," I agreed. "He really is."

"I take it he's here on the island to help you figure out what happened to that poor girl who was found dead in Alex's pool?"

"As far as I can tell that seems to be his purpose, although we haven't made much progress so far."

"Everything in its own time." Father Kilian stood up. "I should let you get inside. The kids should be arriving any minute."

"Yeah, I guess I will head in."

It was so odd for me to know that one day, if things went as planned, Father Kilian would be my uncle. Don't get me wrong; I'm thrilled, but I couldn't help but wonder how rocky the path would be from here to there. I wanted my aunt to finally have the love she had put on hold for so long, but I also didn't want the church that had been almost like a second home to me thrust into conflict and confusion.

Ebenezer seemed to be in his element in the choir room. The only problem with him attending choir practice was that the kids all wanted to play with him rather than rehearse. I understood they were thrilled to see the cat who'd first shown up at choir practice on a snowy December night six months ago, but I was worried that the new song we hoped to showcase was going to be a disaster.

"Okay, everyone. I need you to turn your attention to the front of the room. We have a short rehearsal tonight and we want to get this song down as good as we can before Sunday."

"Can Ebenezer come to practice again next week?" one of the kids asked.

"I'm not sure what Ebenezer's schedule will be."

"He has his own schedule?" one of the boys asked.

"Actually, he does. Very much so. If you all give me a hundred percent effort while we rehearse the new song, there might be time to play with Ebenezer after we finish."

"Where's Mr. Cody tonight?" Trinity Paulson asked.

I frowned. "I'm not sure. He called to say he'd be late, but I know he plans to be here, so let's just start without him. Now, remember to pause for two beats before you segue into the second verse."

"Did you find the dog my dad said you were looking for?" one of the younger boys asked. His father worked for the refuse company, so I'd provided him with a flyer and asked for his help.

"No, not yet. It seems she's afraid of strangers, so no one has been able to catch her."

"My dog likes anyone who gives him food. Maybe you should tell people to bring food with them if they want to catch her."

"Good thinking. I'll mention it the next time I speak to someone who's seen her but couldn't catch her. Remember to sing from your diaphragm."

The kids actually did a good job once I got them on track, which was fortunate because Cody never did show up to help.

He texted to let me know he'd gotten held up and would meet me at the cabin when he was done. Once all the kids were picked up I loaded Ebenezer into the car and headed home. This wasn't the first time Cody had been delayed while researching a story and I was sure it wouldn't be the last, but I hoped he'd make it for our powwow that evening; four brains were definitely better than three.

"Where's Cody?" Siobhan asked when I got inside.

"He got held up. Where's Finn?"

"He had to respond to an accident. It sounded pretty bad. In fact, that might be where Cody is. From what Finn said someone ran a car off the road near Shell Beach and it went through the barrier and over the cliff into the ocean."

I set my backpack on the counter. "Wow. That does sound bad. I can see why Cody would want to cover it. Do we know the condition of the people involved?"

"I'm not sure. The accident happened a while ago, so I bet Finn and Cody will both be here soon. I was thinking about making everyone some dinner rather than going for takeout."

"Sounds good," I agreed. "I think I have everything on hand for a cheesy chicken casserole. I'll text Cody to tell him not to bother stopping to pick anything up."

As it turned out, Finn and Cody arrived just minutes before it was time to take the casserole Siobhan had whipped up out of the oven. In a way it was odd that she was such a good cook because as far as I knew, she never bothered. I don't remember her wanting to spend time in the kitchen when we were children, and she used to joke that she'd never once used the kitchen in her apartment in Seattle. I guess some people just have a natural knack for things whether they practice them or not.

"So what happened?" Siobhan asked Finn as we sat down for our meal.

"According to witnesses, a black sedan swerved into oncoming traffic, causing a car to swerve in order to avoid a head-on collision. The car hit the barrier, which gave way, and the car went over the cliff."

"And the people inside?" I asked.

"Only one person: Brittany Walters."

"Oh God. Is she okay?"

"She's pretty beaten up, but she'll live," Finn said. "Luckily, the spectators responded right away and got her out of the car before she drowned."

"Wow, poor Brittany," I sympathized. "That must have been terrifying."

"Here's the interesting thing," Finn continued. "When I inspected it after she was airlifted to the hospital I found evidence I believe will prove the guardrail was tampered with sometime before the accident."

"Tampered with?" I asked.

"The metal had been partially cut though, weakening it. I know it seems like a long shot, but at this point I'm going to go out on a limb and say it wasn't an accident at all."

The four of us sat in complete silence as we let the significance of that sink in. First Daisy was killed and Alex was drugged and framed. Shortly after that, Val was beaten up and Brittany was run off the road. What in the heck had happened at that party that would cause so many people who were there to be attacked?

"Did anyone see who was driving the car that ran Brittany off the road?" I asked.

"Everyone said the car was black with tinted windows, but no one noticed anything about the driver. One of the witnesses did get a partial license plate that's being run. All we can do right now is continue to investigate and hope something will pop."

"Do you have to go back to San Juan Island tomorrow?" Siobhan asked.

"Unfortunately I do. Tomorrow should be the last day, though."

"After we eat let's take a look at the murder board," she suggested. "I know it seems as if we don't have anything, but sometimes looking back at everything might help us see a pattern."

Cody and I did the dishes while Finn made some calls and Siobhan updated the murder board. The deeper we got into the investigation, the more worried I became for Alex's safety when he was released from jail. I'd thought I wanted him out, but now I was beginning to think he was better off right where he was.

"Okay, here's what we have," Siobhan jumped in as soon as we were all seated in the living room. "There were nine other people at the party at the time Alex went up to his room. Of those nine, Daisy is dead, Val has been assaulted, and Brittany has been run off the road. If we assume the killer has been behind all these incidents, it looks as if we can cross those three off the suspect list. Not that Daisy was ever on it."

"Which brings us to six." I nodded.

"In addition, we've spoken to Connor and Mallery, both of whom claimed to have left the party early. According to Connor, Dirk also left early, which leaves Nick, Stephanie, and Eric as suspects."

"If we believe everyone is telling the truth," I murmured.

"That's the assumption I'm operating on for the benefit of this discussion. We may find later that we need to reevaluate that assumption, but let's go with it for now. And there are also the two older men Connor mentioned," Siobhan added. "I'm adding them to the whiteboard as Unknown One and Unknown Two for the time being."

"Any word at all on Nick?" I asked Finn.

"Not so far. He seems to have disappeared off the face of the earth."

Cody spoke up. "I'm sure he has the means at his disposal to disappear if he wants to. At this point we should probably focus on the suspects we have access to. Someone has to remember something."

"Finn, did you find any other photos on Val's phone that could tell us something?"

"There were several others taken at the party. The photo of Daisy in the pool is the last one she took."

"Maybe the two unknowns are in the previous photos," I suggested.

"I thought of that and checked, but they weren't. Val seemed to be focused on Nick. Almost all the photos had him as the main focal point. Still, it might not hurt to have additional eyes look at them. Someone might see something I didn't notice."

"Do you have them with you?" I asked.

"I have them on my laptop, which is in the car. Hang on; I'll get it."

I noticed Max staring at his empty dish and decided to feed him and Ebenezer while we waited for Finn to return. This entire case was giving me a bad feeling in the pit of my stomach. A young girl being murdered was bad enough, but after what had happened to Val and Brittany I was really worried. If not for the grace of God, Alex might have overdosed on the drug he'd been slipped, Val might have died from her head wound, and Brittany might have drowned had there not been bystanders nearby to get her out of the car in a timely manner. We were lucky we didn't have four murders to investigate.

When Finn came back inside he set his computer up on my dining table and we all gathered around. There were ten photos in all, which Finn scrolled through in order. The first was of Nick standing with a group of people including Alex and Mallery, so I assumed it had been taken shortly after Val arrived at the party. The next was of Nick talking to Mallery, followed by one of Nick chatting with Connor and a guy I didn't recognize. Because he was young and Eric Cassidy was the only male from the original guest list I didn't know, I assumed he was the one with Nick and Connor.

There were several more photos of Nick chatting with various people, but Finn was right; I didn't notice any older men anywhere in the background. The final photo, of Daisy in the pool and Alex asleep in the lounge chair, didn't show anyone else outside.

"Can you send me that file?" I asked Finn. "I don't see anything that seems to be relevant, but you never know when something might come up to change that."

No problem. I'll send it, but these photos are for your eyes only. I don't want the fact that we have them getting out."

I turned to look at Cody. "Did you take photos at the scene of Brittany's accident?"

"Yeah, a bunch."

"Are they on your computer?"

"Still in the camera. I'll download them tomorrow and send everyone a file."

"So where does this leave us?" Siobhan asked.

"We need to talk to Stephanie and Eric," I said. "I've never met either of them."

"I'll talk to them," Cody volunteered. "I'll tell them I'm doing an article for the paper. If I don't get anywhere with them Finn can talk to them in an official capacity once he's finished on San Juan Island."

"I know the deputy who's been covering for me has spoken to both of them. According to the report I read, they both claimed to have been drunk and both swear they don't remember a thing."

"Sometimes people will talk to the press when they won't talk to the cops," Cody pointed out. "I'll take a stab at it tomorrow and we can take it from there."

Cody and I decided to take Max for a walk on the beach after Finn and Siobhan left. It was another beautiful night, with a clear, dark sky and millions of stars sparkling overhead. I really needed this quiet moment with just us after the hectic day I'd had, and I suspected Cody needed the serenity of the sea just as much as I did. I pushed my feet into the sand as the cold water washed over my bare feet. There was something about the long days of summer that caused me to feel nostalgic. I could remember the feeling of freedom that came with the last day of school. My friends and I would head to the beach, where we would spend much of the summer soaking up the sun, visiting with friends, and enjoying all that living on an island had to offer. I can still remember the salty feel of my skin and the sound of seagulls circling overhead.

A young couple walked past us going in the opposite direction. Although the land that ran behind the private estates on the peninsula was rarely accessed by anyone other than the people who lived there, technically the beaches were all public so if a person was inclined to walk along the seashore from the public beach down the way, they were more than welcome to do so.

"I know we're supposed to be relaxing, but I'm really worried about everything that's going on," I eventually said.

"Yeah, me too."

"If things had gone differently Brittany might very well have died today. I just can't imagine what possible reason anyone would have to want all these people dead. At first I thought maybe someone had something against Daisy specifically, but now I'm not so sure."

"It could still be about Daisy," Cody mused as a wave crashed to the shore, covering our legs almost to our knees. "If whoever called 911 hadn't done so when they did Alex would most likely have died of a drug overdose, and with the blood on his shirt and the fingerprints on the knife, there probably wouldn't even have been an investigation."

"But he lived," I added.

"Exactly. And now the photos Val took and whatever it is Brittany knows are suddenly dangerous to the killer. So far we've been lucky and Daisy's has been the only death, but it might only be a matter of time before we have another victim. We have to find whoever is responsible before someone else ends up dead."

"I know this is going to sound crazy, but I'll have a chat with Ebenezer. He showed up before Daisy died, but I still think he's here to help us with this case. Logic tells me cats don't understand English, but experience tells me that my logic isn't always correct."

Cody and I continued to walk in silence, each lost in our own thoughts. I hated to ruin this quality time with the man I loved with thoughts of death, so I frantically searched my mind for an alternate topic of conversation.

"Maggie is going to Seattle tomorrow to pick Haley up at the airport," I told him.

"That's wonderful. I bet they're both excited."

"They are. Maggie has missed Haley something awful, and when I spoke to Haley on the phone yesterday she said she's been counting down the hours."

"It's too bad Maggie never married and had children of her own. She obviously enjoys spending time with children."

It was times like this when I wished I could share Maggie's secret with Cody, but I'd promised my aunt I wouldn't. "I think the years just got away from her. Overall, I believe she's been content with her life, although I'm sure she does wonder how things might have been from time to time. I guess it's hard to get through a whole lifetime without any regrets."

"Do you have any?" Cody asked.

"I'm probably too young to have life regrets at this point, but in answer to your question, no, I don't have any thus far. There are some things I would change if I could, like my father dying at such an early age, but if I look at my own actions and only the things I could control, I think I've done okay. How about you? Any regrets?"

Cody stopped walking. He turned so we were face to face. "Honestly? No. But I'm beginning to regret promising Mr. Parsons I'd be home in time to watch a movie with him."

He leaned forward and kissed me.

"Come on," I said, taking his hand. "I'll come with you. In fact, Max and Ebenezer and I will all come. I've been thinking about the comment you made about me staying at your place sometimes. I think this might be a good time to try it out."

Cody smiled. "Yeah?"

"Yeah."

Chapter 8

Friday, June 24

Coffee Cat Books was slammed the next day, so I really hadn't had much time to work on the case. I'd called and talked to Finn, who'd confirmed that Alex was still in jail and Brittany was still in the hospital but was doing fine. Val had been released from the hospital and had gone to stay with a friend in Seattle. Her location there was considered to be confidential because we still believed her mugging was about her presence at the party, not the contents of her purse. Finn had tried to talk to her, but she was sticking to the story that she didn't remember anything about the night Daisy died. Finn had encouraged her to speak to a therapist law enforcement often used when witnesses had a hard time remembering the details of a crime and, in theory at least, she'd agreed to make an appointment.

Cody forwarded me the file of photos he'd taken at the scene of Brittany's accident, but I hadn't had a chance to look at them yet. Staying with Cody the previous night on the third floor had been a wonderful if not somewhat interesting experience. After Cody decided to move back to the island and took up residence in Mr. Parsons's home, he'd moved all the belongings he'd had in storage into the apartment. The thing was, Cody had gone into the Navy right out of high school, so much of the stuff were things you'd find in a teenage boy's bedroom. When he'd asked me to help him redecorate I'd thought it was just a sweet gesture to make me feel more comfortable in his space, but he really did need to update both his furniture and his décor.

"Can you run into the back to see if we have any more vanilla syrup?" Tara asked. There was a line for beverages going out the door and she had three different drinks going at one time.

"Yeah, sure. Anything else while I'm back there?"

"Cream," Destiny, who was running the cash register, called.

"Excuse me, miss, can you tell me where the cozy mysteries are?" a woman in a red sundress asked as I emerged from behind the counter.

"The mysteries are on the ~~back~~ wall and, generally speaking, the books are arranged from top to bottom based on intensity. Really suspenseful thrillers are at the top and cozies are near the bottom. If you need help locating a specific title just let me know."

"I'm just browsing, but thank you."

I headed toward the hallway that led to the back room. It was days like this when I thought we should have hired more than one summer helper, but Tara pointed out that the rush came in waves and we really did need to watch our nickels and dimes if we were going to turn a profit.

Coffee Cat Books was located in the old cannery, which Tara and I had remodeled prior to opening. It was a fantastic location, right on the wharf in the small town of Pelican Bay. When we'd designed the space we'd divided it in three: The coffee bar and the bookstore were located in the front of the building, closest to Main Street, while the cat lounge was at the back, overlooking the marina. The side of the building closest to the wharf was covered in windows, as was the back wall of the cat lounge, where sofas and cozy chairs were arranged so patrons could look out over the water while reading a book, cozy up with one of our cats, and enjoy a cup of coffee or other beverage.

The part of the building where the storage room and office were located was behind the bookstore but on the side of the building without a water view. There was a side door that led out onto a walkway to Main Street, where most deliveries were received. We always kept that side door locked unless we were actually unloading merchandise, but when I passed the door on the way to get the supplies I noticed it had been left open.

Now, it was possible a customer might have left through that door, failing to close it all the way despite the fact that it was marked as an emergency exit only. But with everything that had been going on, I couldn't help but wonder if the fact that the door had been left open a crack might mean something more. I closed and locked it, grabbed the supplies Tara needed, and returned to the front. As soon as things slowed down a bit, I intended to have a look around to see if anything was missing or had been disturbed.

"Excuse me, miss," a young woman with a cheerful smile stopped me when I reentered the main part of the bookstore. "Do you work here?"

"I do. How can I help you?"

"I was looking at your adorable pink mugs. I think they'd make wonderful gifts for the women in my book club, but you only have five on display. Do you have more in the back?"

"I'll check. How many would you like?"

"Fifteen in all."

A quick glance at the inventory in the computer confirmed that we'd had a delivery the previous day and did indeed have additional mugs in the back. The woman wanted to have the mugs individually boxed and wrapped, so by the time I'd completed her order the crowd had thinned out a bit.

"Did either of you open the delivery door for any reason?" I asked Tara and Destiny after my customer left.

"No, not since the mug delivery we received yesterday. Why?" Tara asked.

"When I went into the back to get the syrup I noticed it was cracked open."

Tara frowned. "It had to have been locked last night when we left or the alarm wouldn't have engaged."

"Which means that someone must have come in through the front today and then left through the side door, either accidentally or intentionally leaving it open."

"I didn't see anyone go into the back," Destiny said.

"Yeah, me neither," Tara agreed. "Although it has been busy, so I suppose if someone timed it right it's possible they could have gone into the back and left through there without our noticing."

"Do you think someone stole something and then snuck out that way?" Destiny asked.

"I hope that's all it is. With everything that's happened this week, it did cross my mind that the person who opened the door was after something more," I answered.

"More?" Destiny wondered.

"I don't know. I just have a bad feeling that someone either snuck in the back and went through our stuff looking for information we had regarding Daisy's murder or someone snuck out through the side door intentionally leaving it open so they could come back inside later."

"It was probably someone looking for the bathroom," Tara asserted.

"The door is clearly marked as an emergency exit," I pointed out. "I'm going to go back to take a look around. See if anything's missing or disturbed. Let me know if we get busy again and I'll come back in front."

I decided to check the supply room first. Although it was hard to know for certain whether anything had been taken, there were no obvious signs that the inventory had been disturbed. I then went into the office and took a look around there. On the surface everything seemed to be in order, but I did notice that my backpack was hanging from the middle peg on the board Tara had installed for us to hang our purses on, and I always hang it on the last peg on the left.

I took my backpack down and opened the top so I could check the contents. Everything appeared to be there. My wallet, credit cards, and cash were all accounted for, as was my notebook, pen, hairbrush, and makeup bag. To be honest, I don't even know why I carried a makeup bag because I almost never bothered to apply the stuff, but it made me feel better knowing I had it just in case an opportunity in which looking pulled together was a must.

Luckily, I'd left my laptop at home. There were a lot of days when it would have been among the contents of my backpack. I couldn't see any reason for either Tara or Destiny to have moved the backpack, but it was clear someone had. If they were looking for something chances were they didn't find it.

Tara poked her head in through the door. "Connor Littleman is here to see you."

"Did you move my backpack on the peg board for some reason?"

"No. Why?"

"Someone moved it."

Tara frowned. "Why would anyone move your backpack?"

"I have no idea. I don't keep anything of value inside. Maybe Destiny moved it."

"You can ask her when she gets back from her ten-minute break."

"Did Connor say what he wanted?" I asked.

"No, he just said it was important. There are still quite a few people out front, so why don't you talk to him in here?"

"Okay, send him back."

I offered Connor a seat across the desk from me, then asked him what was on his mind.

"I heard what happened to Brittany. And after Val being mugged, I began to freak out. When I spoke to your sister the other day I shared some of what I know, but not all. I've been thinking about it a lot and I've decided I should come clean. I went over to the sheriff's office, but there's some new guy there. He said Finn won't be back until next week. I didn't feel comfortable talking to the substitute, so I came here."

"Okay." I leaned in. "I'm listening."

"What I told Siobhan was true. I did attend the party as Brittany's guest and I did leave at around midnight. Both Mallery and Dirk left before I did, but everyone else was still there. What I didn't mention to Siobhan was that I overheard Daisy on the phone earlier in the evening. I went outside for some fresh air and heard her voice on the other side of the hedge. I didn't hear anyone else, so I'm pretty sure she was talking on the phone."

"What time was that?"

"I guess around ten-thirty."

"And what did you hear her say?"

"When I first got there she said something about this not being a good time. I assumed either someone wanted to come over or wanted her to meet them somewhere; I'm not sure. I'd had a lot to drink, so I can't swear I've got the exact words, but I do remember her saying things like: 'No, I haven't changed my mind,' and 'Of course I'm still in.' She also said something about timing; that it was off and maybe they should take a step back."

"But you don't have any idea who she was talking to?"

"No. But shortly after she hung up the two older dudes came by and Daisy didn't look happy. Nick pulled her aside and said something to her, and then they argued. I couldn't hear what they were saying, but it seemed obvious they weren't on the same page."

"And then?"

"And then Daisy went upstairs with the two men and I left. I have no idea what happened after that."

I wasn't sure exactly what we could do with the information he'd provided, but it did seem like maybe the men who'd arrived late could be involved in everything that had happened in some way.

"Can you describe those men?"

"They were tall with dark hair. I don't remember any details like eye color. They were both average in build and had on dress slacks and polos."

"Do you remember anything specific at all that could lead to an identity?"

Connor bit his lip. His eyes rolled up into his head as if he were trying to find a memory he'd all but lost.

"One of the guys had a scar. It started at the outside corner of his eye—right, I think—and ran down toward his ear. The other one had his back to me most of the time, so I didn't see his face."

"And the others? Do you remember where they were when you left?"

"Like I said, Alex was upstairs. Once he went up I didn't see him again. And, like I told your sister, Mallery and Dirk left before me. Daisy was upstairs with the two men, and I seem to remember Eric and Stephanie hooking up and heading for the stairs as well. I have no idea where Nick went after he argued with Daisy. I'd been talking to Val and Brittany before I left, so I know they were still there. Val said something about going to find Nick and Brittany mumbled something about heading out herself."

"Okay, thanks. This helps. If you think of anything else please call me."

"I will. I hope you find whoever is doing this to my friends."

"Yeah, me too."

After Connor left I joined Tara and Destiny in the front. The crowd had thinned out and the next ferry wasn't due for another two hours. The passengers from the last one had been enthusiastic shoppers, so there were some bare shelves that needed to be restocked. I grabbed a box of mugs while Tara restocked the coffee bar and Destiny restocked the bookshelves.

"Did you move my backpack for any reason?" I asked Destiny.

"No. Why?"

"Someone moved it."

"Weird."

"Yeah, it is weird. We've been superbusy today and I'm sure there were times when none of us had an eye on the hallway to the back rooms. I guess someone could have been snooping around for something of value to steal."

"That's creepy. We'll need to make more of a point to lock the office."

"I'm sure once we get some extra help we'll be able to monitor the crowd better," I added.

"When is Roni going to start?" Destiny asked.

"Tomorrow, actually," Tara replied.

"That's good. We can really use the help. It's been hard trying to spend time with James and put in extra hours here."

"I realize you've had to make a lot of sacrifices these past couple of weeks and Cait and I really appreciate it. Hopefully we can get you back on a regular schedule next week."

"I'm happy to do what I can after everything you've done for me."

Tara turned her attention to me. "Did Connor have any new information?"

"Yes and no. He remembered a telephone conversation he overheard Daisy having that sounds like it could be relevant, but it's really too vague to be a lot of help. I'm going to call Finn to fill him in. He texted earlier to say he should be on the six-fifteen ferry. At least the trial is over, so he should be able to devote a lot more time to the case."

"Are you all getting together tonight?" Tara asked.

"I'm not sure. Cody's coming over, but I haven't discussed it with Finn and Siobhan. If we do have a mystery meeting do you want to come?'

"Yeah, I'm in."

"How was your date last night?"

Tara smiled. "It was very, very nice."

"Still not going to tell me who it was with?"

"Not quite yet. I know I usually share every little detail of every date with you, but this guy is different. It's a little early to say, but I think there's a possibility that our relationship might actually go somewhere."

The fact that Tara was keeping the identity of her new guy so close to the vest made me more than just a little suspicious. "You aren't hooking up with Danny again?"

"No, it's not Danny."

"Can you at least give me a hint?"

"The guy I'm seeing is a little older than the ones I've dated in the past, and he's intelligent and hardworking and a lot more mature and dependable."

"You haven't hooked up with some geezer old enough to be your father, have you?"

Tara laughed. "No, he's not quite that old. If and when I decide to share with you I promise you'll like him. He's out of town at the moment and will be for another week, so if you have a meeting give me a call."

Someone mature and out of town. This was a small island; I should be able to figure this one out.

Chapter 9

Cody was on the lawn talking to Maggie and Haley when I arrived home, and Haley ran up to my car as soon as she saw me. "I've missed you," she said as she hugged me the minute I stepped out.

"I've missed you too." I hugged her back. "I'm so glad your dad let you come for the summer."

"Me too. It's boring at home, unlike here, which is awesome. Maggie is taking me out to dinner. Do you want to come?"

"I would, but I have some people coming over to my place tonight. We'll do dinner next week for sure."

"Okay."

I looked toward the lawn, where Ebenezer and Max were lying in the shade. "I see you've met Ebenezer."

"I have. He's the smartest cat I've ever seen. I was just talking to him and he seemed to understand."

"Yeah, he's a smart one."

"Maggie said he's here to help you solve a murder."

"That's what I'm hoping. How's your dad doing?" Haley's father had taken it really hard when her mother had died last summer.

"Better. He still misses Mom—we both do—but he seems happier."

"That's good. I worried about both of you after your mom passed. I'm really happy things are going better and I'm really happy to have you here."

Haley hugged me again. "I guess I should go in and change for dinner. Maggie said she's taking me to a nice place."

"Okay. We'll hang out tomorrow."

I watched Haley trot away. The huge grin on her face was infectious. I really *was* glad it had worked out for her to spend the summer with us. Infectious smiles were hard to come by.

"It's nice to have Haley back." Cody kissed me after Maggie and Haley went in and he joined me near the car.

"Yeah, it really is. How was your day?"

"Productive."

"The best kind. Finn, Siobhan, and Tara are coming over, so I bought stuff to BBQ. They should be here any time if you want to start the grill while I butter bread and make a salad."

I called Max and Ebenezer into the cabin and then hurriedly put away the groceries I'd bought. It was going to be a warm evening, so I ran upstairs to change out of my work clothes and into shorts and a tank. Ebenezer jumped up onto the bed and watched as I hung up the capris I'd worn that day. It was nice having a cat in the house again. The ones who showed up to help me never stayed long. While I missed them, I knew their leaving at the end of the investigation was part of the plan, so I tried not to get overly attached. Still, there were times I considered getting an all-the-time cat to share a home with Max and me.

"I spoke to Connor today," I informed Ebenezer. "I'm still not sure what happened, but it seems like the two older men who came by after Alex went to bed could be involved in Daisy's death."

"Meow."

"I know we don't have a lot to go on, but I'm having a hard time figuring out why any of the others at the party would have killed Daisy."

Ebenezer swatted at the backpack I'd tossed on the bed.

"No, I don't have any salmon treats in there."

"Meow."

"Yes, there are some downstairs."

Ebenezer continued to scratch at my backpack.

"I told you, there aren't any treats in there."

The cat scratched harder.

"I'm telling the truth. Look." I opened my backpack so the cat could look inside.

Ebenezer stuck his head into the bag and pulled out my makeup bag.

"It's just makeup. Very old makeup, considering I rarely wear it. I promise you, there's nothing in there you would want."

"Meow."

I let out a long breath. "Look." I unzipped the bag. "No treats."

Ebenezer swatted the bag out of my hand, causing it to fall to the floor. Some of the contents fell out onto the floor, and I bent down to pick it up, only to find a compact I didn't recognize. It looked like powder, but it wasn't mine. I remembered the break-in at the store. Could someone have put the compact in my bag? Why would anyone do that?"

"It's a tracking device," Finn informed me when he arrived.

"A tracking device?"

"A GPS. Similar to the ones in your cell phone. If someone put this in your bag that means they wanted to keep an eye on your movements."

"Oh my God. Do you think Cait is this madman's next target?" Siobhan cried.

"I don't know if the person wants to kill her, but he definitely wanted to follow her."

"So whoever planted the device knew the backpack belonged to Cait," Cody said. "And not only did they know the backpack belonged to her but that she had a bag with makeup inside that she never wore, so she'd most likely never even notice the device."

"In other words it was planted by someone who knows Cait well," Siobhan whispered, the fear evident in her voice.

"That actually makes sense," Tara added. "For someone to have snuck into the back they would have had to have been familiar to us. Someone we wouldn't feel we needed to keep an eye on."

"Okay, so who was in the store today?" Finn asked.

"A lot of people," I said. "We had a busy day. The store was packed most of the time. There's no way to determine who might have snuck into the back room to plant the device."

"I'm going to hang on to it," Finn told them. "Maybe I can pull a print or something."

"The steaks are almost done," Cody said. "Let's go ahead and eat and then we can all share whatever news we've gathered since last night."

There was a temporary lull in the conversation as we got dinner on the table. It was another beautiful day in paradise, and we all gathered around the picnic table on the deck overlooking the sea. Danny would be working late pretty much every night until the weather cooled and the whales left, so I doubted we'd be seeing much of him from this point forward. My mother hated the fact that both Danny and Aiden tended to miss our Sunday meals once the fishing season really kicked into gear, which is why I went out of my way not to miss the weekly event. It made me sad to think that those family dinners would end when Mom married and moved away. Of course if Cassie moved in with Siobhan and Maggie, the dinners would simply move from Mom's house to Maggie's.

I watched Rambler as he chased Max down the beach. Watching the dogs play filled me with a certain contentment, even if the fact that someone had slipped a tracking device into my bag was worrying me just a bit.

"I guess it's a good thing we're enjoying the weather while we can," Cody said. "According to the National Weather Service there's a storm blowing in this weekend."

I looked out at the perfectly blue sky and the deep aqua sea. "Really? It's so nice. It feels like summer has finally arrived."

"It's just supposed to be a short storm. No more than twenty-four hours, beginning tomorrow night. But it's also supposed to be pretty intense, so you might want to tie down your deck furniture. I heard we're apt to have sixty-mile-an-hour winds with even stronger gusts."

"Figures," I grumbled. "I just got everything set out and now I'll need to put it all away."

"I brought some tie-downs," Cody reassured me. "I'll secure everything before I leave."

I smiled. He really was the best boyfriend. He seemed to anticipate my needs and take care of them before I even knew I had them.

"So, now that we've devoured the food you and Cait made, why don't you tell us what you learned today," Siobhan suggested. She'd been fidgety throughout dinner. Clearly she was as worried about the fact that someone had set out to track me as I was.

"Okay." Cody set his napkin aside. "Let's go inside where we can refer to the murder board."

We all got up and did as Cody suggested. Once we were settled Cody began to fill us in.

"I spoke with Stephanie Young and Eric Cassidy today. They both said the reason they were at the party in the first place was because they were hanging out at O'Malley's when Brittany got an invite to the party from Nick. Nick told Brittany she could bring people if she wanted, so she just invited everyone sitting near her. Prior to that evening neither Stephanie nor Eric knew Brittany, and neither of them knew each other. Eric was at the bar alone after a long day at work; Stephanie was with Val."

So far this fit what we'd already been told by the other people we'd interviewed.

"Eric and Stephanie both admitted they hooked up with each other at the party. Eric said that at some point he fell asleep and didn't awake until Stephanie found Daisy floating in the pool. He said Stephanie called 911 and then they both left. Stephanie said much the same thing.

She said she and Eric both fell asleep but that she woke up and was thirsty. When she went downstairs the place was deserted. She went out onto the patio to see if anyone was around and saw Daisy floating in the pool and Alex passed out in the lounge chair with blood on his shirt. She woke up Eric, called 911 from the house phone, and they left."

"So either they're lying or the killer had already gone by the time Stephanie went down for a drink."

"That was my conclusion as well," Cody confirmed.

"Where was everyone else?" I asked.

"Good question," Siobhan agreed.

"I don't know where everyone went during the time Eric and Stephanie were upstairs, but I do have the location of everyone earlier in the evening," I shared. "After I spoke to Connor today I jotted down a timeline of the evening's events, at least according to him. At the time he left, around midnight, Alex had gone upstairs, Mallery and Dirk had left, Stephanie and Eric were upstairs hooking up, Daisy was upstairs with the men who'd shown up later, and Val and Brittany were in the living room chatting. I figure Daisy didn't kill herself, and right now I'm going to continue to believe Alex didn't do it, which leaves the men who came later, Val, Brittany, Stephanie, and Eric. Val and Brittany have both been assaulted, and if we believe Eric and Stephanie, that leaves our mystery men as the logical killers."

"We need to find out who they are," Siobhan stated the obvious.

None of us were sure where to begin doing that, so we all sat in silence staring at the murder board as if by some sort of magic a solution would appear. I guess Ebenezer must have gotten tired of our slow progress because he got up off the couch and jumped up onto the kitchen table, where my laptop was sitting. He pawed at it until I got up and logged on. Sitting right there on the desktop was the file with the photos Cody had sent me. We'd been so busy all day that I'd never had a chance to look at them. Now I opened the file and began to sift through it. The photos had been taken at the scene of Brittany's accident, and there were photos of the car in the water, rescue personnel tending to Brittany, and the crowd that had gathered to watch. Brittany had been rescued by a group of surfers who were in the area when the car went over the cliff. It occurred to me that Brittany must have had a tracking device on her body as well for the killer to know the exact moment to approach from the opposite lane.

At first I didn't think the photos would help us at all, but Ebenezer seemed to want me to look at them and I had to assume the silly cat had a reason for doing so. Then I noticed something that previously had seemed so insignificant that I would have missed it if I hadn't been looking so closely.

"Look at this guy in the back of the crowd." I pointed to a spot on the screen in front of me. "The tall guy with the dark hair. Doesn't it look like he has a scar on his face?"

Finn, Cody, and Siobhan squeezed in behind me.

"I don't know; it's hard to tell," Cody commented.

"And his dark glasses are concealing part of his face," Siobhan added.

"I suppose it could be a scar," Finn said. "But it could also be a shadow or a trick of the light. Why do you ask?"

I explained that Connor had said that one of the men he'd overheard arguing with Daisy had had a scar on his face from the corner of his eye to his ear. It really was hard to tell if the man in the photo had a matching scar, but at this point we didn't have much to go on, so I figured it wouldn't hurt to check it out further. Cody had state-of-the-art photography equipment at the newspaper, so we all piled into cars to head into town so Cody could try to isolate the man and blow up the cropped image.

Once Cody had done what he could with the photo, Finn drove over to Connor's and showed him the photo. Connor told Finn he wasn't 100 percent certain the man at the accident was the same one he'd seen at the party, though it definitely could have been. After they finished we all headed to Finn's office to thumb through mug shots.

"Even if the man at the scene of the accident is the guy who showed up at the party, he can't be the one who slipped the compact into Cait's backpack, which, to be honest, is the thing that has me the most worried," Siobhan said.

"I agree with Siobhan," Tara seconded. "I've been racking my brain trying to come up with a list of suspects, but there were a lot of people in the store today. I'm fairly certain no one from the party came in."

"Besides, we already decided that whoever slipped the compact into Cait's backpack must have known her pretty well," Siobhan added.

"Did you know anyone at the party well enough for them to know you carried a backpack and kept makeup inside?" Cody asked.

"Alex. When he worked for us last December I dipped into my makeup stash to give Santa rosy cheeks. Alex also knew I preferred a backpack to a purse, but Alex is in jail and I don't see any reason he'd want to hurt me."

"Anyone else?" Cody asked.

"I guess maybe Val. We were pretty close in high school and I carried a backpack back then too. But again, I don't see why she'd want me dead."

"At this point we're assuming whoever slipped the compact into your backpack did so because they wanted to harm you," Finn said. "We don't know that for certain."

"Hey, I think I have something," Tara interrupted. She pointed to a photo in the book she was looking through. "Doesn't this look like our guy? He has the same scar as the man in the other photo."

Finn held up the photo Cody had enhanced next to the one in the book. "It looks like this could be the same guy. His name is Jimmy Gregory. He's a conman who's best known for working for other people. I'll run his profile to see if I can find out what he's been up to."

We all waited while Finn pulled up Gregory's rap sheet. Even if the man at the accident was the same one Connor saw at the party we still needed to figure out how he was connected to Daisy and why he would have wanted her dead.

Siobhan, Tara, Cody, and I chatted about the upcoming Fourth of July events while Finn worked to dig up what he could on Gregory.

"It looks like Gregory was in prison until a month ago. He's out on parole and isn't supposed to leave the state of Oregon, so if he's the man who was at the party, he was violating his parole just by being there."

"Why was Gregory in prison in the first place?" I wondered.

"He was involved in a con focused on wealthy elderly people. He worked with a partner to convince these seniors to invest in their project, which was supposed to be guaranteed to double their money, but the whole thing was a scam. He served less than half of his sentence before being released on good behavior. He checked in with his parole officer two days before showing up at Alex's party."

"And Jimmy's partner from that scam? Could it have been the man he was with at the party?" I asked.

"No. Jimmy's partner is still in prison. He must have hooked up with someone new."

"I guess a party at a rich kid's house might be a good target for a con man," Cody offered.

"Yeah, but why would Daisy be involved with someone intent on scamming her friends?" Tara asked.

"Good question," I agreed.

"And the people who happened to be at the party that night weren't Alex and Nick's usual crowd," Siobhan added. "In fact, the only person there with money besides them was Daisy."

"Connor did say it seemed Daisy was telling the person on the phone that the timing was wrong," I reminded everyone. "Maybe Gregory didn't believe her and showed up anyway. When he got to the party and found out that there were no rich kids to scam he got mad and killed Daisy."

I could tell by the looks of doubt on everyone's faces that no one bought that scenario, and to be honest, it seemed like a stretch to me as well.

"I should get going," Tara said. "I have a feeling we're going to be slammed at the bookstore tomorrow."

"Yeah, I should get going too," I seconded.

"I'll keep digging," Finn assured us. "Don't worry; we'll get whoever is behind all this." He looked at me. "In the meantime, be careful."

"Count on it."

Chapter 10

Sunday, June 26

Sunday dinner at Mom's turned out to consist of my younger sister Cassidy and me eating with Mom while she complained about every little detail of the wedding, which somehow wasn't coming together the way she'd envisioned. Aiden and Danny were both fishing and Siobhan claimed to have come down with a terrible migraine, although if you asked me, it was her shopping excursion with Mom the previous day that had given her the headache in the first place.

"How about we go out to dinner because it's just us," I suggested as soon as it became apparent that Aunt Maggie was otherwise occupied as well.

"I guess it would be nice not to have to cook," Mom answered. "Trying to get ready for a wedding the size of the one Reginald and I are planning has become almost more than I can manage."

"You could postpone it," Cassie suggested. "Or even cancel it altogether. There's not a person in town who wouldn't understand."

"No, I couldn't do that. Reginald is looking forward to a big wedding. I'm sure once I get things organized I'll be able to relax and have a wonderful time."

"Can we make it an early dinner?" Cassie inquired. "I'd like to hang out with my friends later."

I looked at Mom. "I could eat now."

"Sure. Just let me grab my purse."

Cassie and I knew that *grab my purse* was code for *fix my hair, freshen my makeup, and change my clothes*, so we headed out onto the back patio and sat on the swing overlooking the yard.

"I can't believe Mom is going to sell this house," Cassie said, obvious grief in her voice. Mom had dropped this bombshell on us earlier in the day, when I'd suggested Siobhan might just stay in the house with Cassie until she turned eighteen. "It's almost as much a part of the family as the people who've lived in it."

"I've been having a problem with the whole thing as well. It's bad enough that she's leaving the island, but I can't imagine another family in this house."

"Dad is probably turning over in his grave at the way things turned out."

I hated to think of my dad being upset by the situation even if he was in heaven and probably removed from the outcome, but Cassie was right; Dad wouldn't have approved of Mom selling the house. When she'd first said she was moving I'd assumed Aiden would continue to live in it whether Cassie stayed or not, but Mom said she needed the money and the house had appreciated so much in value over the years that there was no way Aiden could afford to buy it from her.

"Maybe we can help Aiden figure out a way to buy the house," I suggested.

"Why should he have to buy it? It's as much his house as anyone's. You know Dad intended for it to be handed down when the time came."

"I agree. That *is* what Dad intended, but Mom insists she needs the money."

Cassie kicked her legs out so that we started to swing. "Why? I thought the jerk Mom is marrying is rich. Doesn't he plan to support her once they're married?"

I agreed with Cassie. Why was Mom so desperate for money that she'd sell the house all five of her children were born and raised in if the man she was marrying was as loaded as he'd led everyone to believe?

"And if Mom is so broke what's up with the huge wedding?" she added. "I can't even begin to imagine how much this whole thing must be costing. Did you know Mom is paying for everything?"

"She is?"

"I overheard her arguing with Aiden before he left to go fishing. Between the wedding and the money she's spent on the guy she's burned through half her savings. Aiden tried to tell her that she should talk to Reginald about paying some of the expenses, but Mom insists the wedding is the bride's responsibility and she doesn't want to bother him with the whole thing."

"That's crazy."

"Right! Mom has lost her mind. We need to do something before it's too late."

I hadn't been thrilled with Mom's plan to marry a man we barely knew from the beginning, but now I was really concerned. Dad had left Mom with enough money to support her for the rest of her life, so if what Cassie said was true and she had burned through half her money we were talking about a significant dollar amount. And the house where we'd all been brought up was paid for. There was a time when real estate on the island wasn't worth all that much, but with the arrival of the ferry and the increase in tourism, property values had increased dramatically. I was sure it was safe to say that the six-bedroom house was worth close to a million dollars in this market.

Mom joined us on the patio. "Are you girls ready?"

"Yeah, we're ready," I answered. "Antonio's?"

"Where else would we go?" Antonio's had been a family favorite for as long as I could remember.

The three of us sat quietly while we made the drive into Harthaven. I still couldn't get over the idea that everything was going to change so dramatically.

"It looks like the storm Cody told me about on Friday has finally arrived about twelve hours late," I commented as raindrops began to hit the windshield.

"Where's Cody anyway?" Cassie asked.

"He wanted to spend some time with Mr. Parsons and I had plans to spend the day with you, so it seemed like a good time."

The parking lot at Antonio's was only half full, but it was early for dinner and late for lunch so it shouldn't be crowded. I parked as close to the door as I could and the three of us made a dash through the rain toward the entrance. Mom chose a seat near the window, which allowed me to monitor the comings and goings at the front door. I guess the fact that someone had slipped a tracking device into my bag had spooked me more than I realized because I found myself looking over my shoulder a lot more than I normally did. Finn hadn't been able to grab any prints off the compact, so we still didn't know who had planted it.

During our marathon day at the bookstore yesterday Tara and I had both kept going to check the side door. By the end of the day Tara had suggested calling the alarm company and having them alarm the door individually so if anyone tried to open it in the future an alarm would sound, alerting us. She also suggested we might want to invest in a surveillance system. We'd talked about one when we first opened, but with our budget it was one of the things that ended up on the chopping block.

Of course the idea of a surveillance system made me wonder about the one at the house where Daisy had died. I'd tried to get in touch with Balthazar Pottage that morning to see if he'd installed one when he remodeled the house, but he hadn't answered the phone and, so far, hadn't called me back.

"Well, this is nice," Mom commented after we'd given the waitress our orders. "I do love our big family dinners, but I also enjoy having just my two youngest to dote on."

"Guess there won't be any more doting once you move," Cassie grumbled.

"Nonsense. I'm not moving across the world. Newport Beach is really just a short flight away. I'll be home for all the special occasions."

"Speaking of special occasions, I wanted to add Reginald to my birthday calendar because he's going to be a member of the family, but I don't know that you ever told us his birthday," I commented.

Mom frowned. "You know, I'm not sure it's ever come up. I'll find out and let you know."

"You're marrying a man and you don't even know his birthday?" Cassie demanded.

I kicked Cassie under the table. I figured this dinner was as good a time as any to try to find out more about the guy and Mom wasn't going to share if we put her on the defensive.

"What Cassie means is that it's funny how we can forget to ask about the little details when we first enter into a relationship," I covered for her.

"Yes, well, it is true that there are many things you would think you'd know that simply haven't come up. Like the other day I wanted to send Reginald a sample of the linens I'd chosen for the tables and I realized I didn't have his mailing address."

"I bet he thought that was funny when you called him to ask."

A strange look came over Mom's face, but she shook it off. "I actually never got hold of him. I left a message on his cell, but he hasn't called me back. I'm sure he's much too busy getting his banking disaster figured out to worry about linens."

"Banking disaster?" I leaned in closer.

"Apparently, someone stole his identity and they froze all his assets until they got it sorted out. Reginald was pretty upset about the fact that his assets were frozen at first because he had no way to pay his bills, but I assured him I'd wire him some money so he could get by for a few weeks. I'm sure things will get straightened out shortly."

Cassie met my eyes and I silently warned her not to say anything. "I think

I'll use the ladies' room before our meal comes," I said.

"Me too." Cassie stood.

As soon as we were out of earshot, Cassie pulled me to one side. "Did you hear that?"

"I'm going to call Finn. For the time being don't say anything else to put Mom on the defensive. Let's play along with her fantasy and see what we can find out."

"Okay," Cassie agreed. "I'll follow your lead."

Over the course of the meal we learned how very little Mom actually knew about Reginald. They'd met on the cruise and he'd swept her off her feet. After she arrived home flowers and small gifts began arriving in the mail. After a few weeks he told Mom he was going to be in Seattle on business and asked if she'd like to join him. During that visit he'd wined and dined her, and just before she left to come home he'd proposed and she'd accepted. The only other time they'd spent together was when he came to the island so she could make her big announcement to us. I asked her if she spoke to him often and she said they chatted on the phone from time to time.

She admitted that while she'd seen photos of his home she'd never actually been there, and that he really never talked much about his family or his life outside the time they spent together. She told us she figured she had plenty of time to get to know him better after they were wed. Cassie asked her why the wedding was taking place so soon after their meeting and Mom said Reginald felt life was short and that neither of them were spring chickens, so they needed to act fast to have the most time together.

I'll confess that I ordered a bottle of wine and kept Mom's glass filled. That may seem like a conniving thing for a daughter to do, but I figured this might be my only chance to get to the bottom of what was going on and I wanted her as relaxed and open as possible.

The idea to sell the house had come from Reginald, which I'd suspected all along. He'd pointed out to Mom that they wouldn't need it after she moved in with him.

"I know it seems as if Reginald has left me to do all the work for the wedding, but he's helping as well. He's taking care of all the financial stuff, which you know I hate."

That much was true. Mom did hate dealing with the finances, which was why Aiden took care of them for her.

"Taking care of the financial stuff how?" I asked.

"He's setting up joint accounts, investments, insurance, everything. Isn't that nice?"

"Have you transferred any of your money into those accounts yet?" I asked.

"No. I'm waiting for Aiden to get home from fishing. To be honest, other than my checking account I have no idea where Aiden stashed the money Dad left me."

Well, that at least was good. It sounded like a second call to Finn as well as a call to Aiden's voice mail was in order.

After I drove Mom and Cassie home I headed to the cabin to get Max. It was raining steadily, but I couldn't get the thought of actually going over to Alex's house and looking around out of my mind. And I wouldn't even have to break in. Balthazar Pottage had given me a key so I could let the contractors in when the house had been undergoing renovation. He'd even given me the code to the alarm system once it was activated. The house was isolated and it was getting late, so chances were no one would be around to know I'd been there.

Chapter 11

By the time I got home the storm was intensifying so I changed into a pair of jeans and a sweatshirt. I pulled on a worn pair of Nikes and secured my long, curly hair in a band. I grabbed my backpack and called Max to come with me before opening the door and venturing out into the wind and rain. I was about to pull away from my cabin when I noticed Ebenezer sitting in the window, so I ran back into the cabin and grabbed the cat as well. You never knew, after all, when a magical cat might come in handy.

The house his father had given Alex was located on the north end of the island. The property had highway access, but the house itself was built out on the point, which required a fairly long ride on the private drive. I pulled up in front of the dark house and said a silent prayer that Alex hadn't changed the locks since moving in. Thunder rumbled in the distance as Max, Ebenezer, and I ran for the front door.

"Oh good, the key still works." I opened the door and hurried across the entry to the keypad to turn off the alarm only to find it hadn't been set. I went back to close the front door behind my furry friends, who were shaking the rain from their fur.

I looked around the large hall, trying to decide where to begin my search. There were two stories linked by a single staircase, which was wide and opened into the main living area of the lower floor, which also housed the kitchen and several bedrooms. I figured Alex, Nick, and Daisy would all have taken the larger suites on the second floor, so I decided to begin my search up there.

The house was littered with empty cups and half-full beer bottles. It was clear no one had been in to clean up after the murder. I turned on the light over the staircase. It was still several hours until sunset, but the storm had blocked out the light from the sun almost completely. As I slowly made my way up the stairs I found myself hoping no one had decided to stay at the house in Alex's absence. Alex had hosted a steady flow of friends since he'd been on the island and it was possible he had given someone else, like the still missing Nick, a key.

The first suite I checked must have been lived in by Daisy; there were female garments in the closet, as well as cosmetics and female toiletries in the bathroom. The room had a separate seating area which, based on the crumbs on the sofa and the half-empty glasses, looked like it had been occupied the night of the party. Odd that the deputy who'd investigated the crime hadn't taken the glasses away to check for fingerprints. I noticed there were rings of moisture on the table that were still wet, which was when I realized the glasses had been placed there more recently than a week ago.

"Someone has been staying here," I said to Max and Ebenezer, who were following me around the room. I guessed that explained why the alarm hadn't been set. Whoever had been here most likely planned to return shortly.

"Well?" I asked Ebenezer when I didn't see anything that immediate looked like a clue.

Ebenezer headed to the door and then trotted down the hall. The next room we entered also looked like it had been occupied recently. There were towels in the bathroom that were still damp and a newspaper with yesterday's date on it sitting on the coffee table in front of the sofa in the seating area. The clothes in the closet looked too large to belong to Alex, so I had to believe this was Nick's room. Could he still be using the room under the radar?

Thunder cracked in the distance and the wind picked up, causing the house to shake as each gust slammed into it. I just hoped the electricity didn't give out, though if there was someone living in the house turning on the lights as I made my way through probably wasn't the best idea either.

The room at the end of the hall was the largest one in the house and the one I assumed Alex had taken for himself. Unlike the other two, there was no sign of a recent occupant. I stood in the center of the room and tried to decide what it was I was looking for. I'd come out to the house on a whim and was notably short of a plan, but I had a feeling in my gut that there was something here for me to find if only I knew where to look.

I kept coming back to the fact that so far we really hadn't uncovered a motive for Daisy's death and Alex's drugging. The only thing that made sense was that the two men who'd shown up late were responsible for both, but who were they and why had they done what they had? I'd just begun to open the nightstand drawer when I heard a crash coming from downstairs. Damn; whoever was living here must have come home. My first thought was to flee, but the only way out of the house was down the stairs and most likely into the arms of the intruder, so I pulled my phone out of my pocket and called Finn.

"Hey, Cait, what's up?"

"I'm at Alex's," I whispered.

"What in tarnation are you doing there?"

I heard another crash. I made my way over to the window and looked out. I didn't see another car in the drive. Maybe the crashing had been caused by the wind if someone had left a window open. Then I heard a door slam. Or maybe not.

"You can read me the riot act later. Max, Ebenezer, and I are upstairs. I can hear someone downstairs."

"Hide. I'm on my way."

I put my phone back into my pocket and looked at the animals. "What do you think? Under the bed or in the closet?"

Ebenezer trotted into the bathroom and I followed. I looked at the shower. "Oh no. I've seen this movie. There's no way I'm getting in there."

I noticed a door next to the shower. Most likely it belonged to a linen closet. I opened it for good measure and realized the door covered the old dumbwaiter. The system used to lead into the smaller bedroom of the master suite, but with the remodel, that room had been used to increase the size of the bathroom. I thought Balthazar had taken out the dumbwaiter system when he redid the place, but apparently he hadn't. I was pretty small, but I doubted I could fit into the small space, especially if I was accompanied by a cat and a dog.

"Good thinking," I said to Ebenezer, "but it's too small for all of us."

I could hear someone on the stairs. They weren't trying to be quiet, so I guessed they figured they had the upper hand against an intruder. Ebenezer jumped into the dumbwaiter and meowed.

"You want me to lower you down?"

"Meow."

I didn't see how that would help, but I had nothing to lose, so I did what he wanted. I wasn't sure he'd be able to manage the door to get out when he got downstairs, but it must have been open because the next thing I heard was a huge crash from the kitchen.

"Who's there?" the man on the stairs called out.

I realized this was my opportunity to escape, so Max and I snuck down the stairs and out the front door while the man downstairs went into the kitchen to investigate the source of the crash. I jumped into my car and drove away. I couldn't risk waiting for Ebenezer, but I prayed the entire time that he was okay.

When I got to the end of the private drive I stopped and waited. The rain was coming down in sheets, and as hard as I tried I was having a hard time keeping an eye out for anyone coming down the drive. Finn pulled up just as I was beginning to panic. He rolled down his window and I rolled down mine and explained what was going on. He insisted that I head home before he shifted his car into gear and headed down the drive toward the house.

I'd caused enough trouble for one night, so I did as Finn demanded and headed home.

"What's taking so long?" I complained to Cody, who'd come over as soon as I called him to fill him in.

"I don't know; was Finn alone?"

I nodded. "Should we go out to Alex's place to check on things? What if he's in trouble?"

Cody looked uncertain and I didn't blame him. On one hand, Finn was a cop and trained for this type of situation; on the other, we didn't know who'd been waiting for him in the house.

"I'm sure he called for backup before he went inside," Cody said, attempting to comfort me.

"I didn't see anyone following him. I'm going. If nothing else, I can call 911 if it looks like Finn's in trouble."

I was just preparing to leave my cabin when Finn pulled up. I let out the breath it felt like I'd been holding ever since I'd first heard the noise downstairs in Alex's house. I was even more relieved when I saw Ebenezer jump out of the car after Finn.

"My God, I was so worried. What took you so long?"

"I had to wait until someone got there to take the intruder to jail."

"You could have called," I scolded him.

"I was a little busy. Besides, I didn't think you'd be worried. Most of the time people stop worrying as soon as the cops get there."

"So who was it? Who was in the house?"

Finn was totally wet from head to toe. "I have a change of clothes in my trunk. Let me dry off and get into some dry clothes and I'll fill you both in."

I put on some coffee while Cody built a fire. Despite the warm temperatures we'd been enjoying, the storm had brought a chill to the air.

"Is Finn here?" Siobhan shook the moisture from her umbrella as she came in my side door.

"He's putting on some dry clothes. Come on in and I'll catch you up while we wait."

By the time I'd explained about going to Alex's house and discovering someone was staying there Finn returned to the living room.

"So?" I asked. "What happened?"

"What happened is that you came very close to being killed tonight. What were you thinking?"

"I don't know," I admitted. "I was home alone and I started thinking about things and remembered I had a key to Alex's house, and I figured it was empty, so what was the harm in looking around?"

"I think you took a year off my life when you called to tell me you were in the house. You never should have gone out there by yourself."

I could see Finn was really mad. Madder than I'd seen him in a very long time.

"I'm sorry. But it turned out okay."

"Thanks to your cat. I let you help me with these cases because I thought you had a good head on your shoulders and would use caution and common sense. If you're going to go off on these tangents I'm afraid we're done working together."

Geez. I really had blown it.

"I'm sorry. I really am. I did a stupid thing and it won't happen again."

Finn still looked mad, but at least he'd stopped yelling.

"So did you get the guy?" I finally asked.

"Yeah, I got him."

"We caught Daisy's killer? Alex can get out of jail?"

"I'm afraid it's a bit more complicated than that."

"Okay; I'm listening."

"The person you heard in the house was Nick Farmer, only that isn't really his name; it's Nick Madison."

"I wondered what happened to him."

"Like Alex, Nick was drugged and left to die. Unlike Alex, his body wasn't discovered, yet despite the amount of drugs in his system, he managed to wake up. The problem was that by the time he came to, Daisy's body had been discovered, Alex was in jail, and there was an all-points bulletin out on him."

"So he went underground," I assumed.

"Exactly."

"Was Daisy even his sister?" Siobhan asked.

"No. Nick confessed that he and Daisy were hired by a man whose name he either really doesn't know or refuses to reveal to get close to Alex. Their mission was to use his money to throw exclusive parties for other rich kids and use them to find dirt that could be used to blackmail them."

"This whole thing was a blackmail scheme?" I asked incredulously.

"So it seems. The problem was that somewhere along the way Daisy started to actually care about Alex. When he didn't want to have a party she went along with it at first, so no party was planned, but the man was having none of it. He contacted Nick to tell him to have a party or else."

"Which is why Nick called people at the last minute," Siobhan stated.

"Exactly. Daisy was unhappy that Alex was upset and called the number they'd been given and told their contact they needed to back off a bit. She told him that she felt Alex might stop having the parties altogether. Daisy could see Alex was agitated, so she gave him something to help him sleep, but she didn't know Nick had tampered with the drug and what she gave him was a double dose that could have killed him."

"And then the thugs showed up," Cody contributed.

"Right. They drugged Nick and left him to die, killed Daisy, and set the scene to make it look as if Alex had killed Daisy. Alex was supposed to die. If he had no one would have questioned it. Nick believes if all three of them had died as planned, the deaths would have been chalked up to a wild party gone bad."

"The fact that Alex and Nick lived definitely complicated things. Did Nick know why Val and Brittany were attacked?' I asked.

"No. He assumes they saw something they shouldn't have, but he's not sure. He's been out of the loop since the night of the murder. He wants his boss and the thugs to think he's dead. Of course now he's in jail."

"And Alex?" I wondered.

"I'm sure he'll be freed, but honestly, I think he's better off where he is right now. Though he has the means to really disappear if he wants to."

"We need to figure out who the other players are and put this whole thing to bed once and for all," I insisted.

"I agree, but it isn't going to be easy. According to Nick, he doesn't know the name of the guy who hired him or what he looks like; the thugs were the go-between. We need to catch them to see if they'll lead us to their boss."

Chapter 12

Monday, June 27

The next morning Cassie called me in hysterics. Reginald had shown up unannounced late the night before. Mom was over-the-moon happy, but Cassie was on the verge of going over the deep end. She asked if I would come pick her up. I texted Tara to let her know I'd be late yet again, and then I grabbed my backpack and headed out the door.

"Can you believe that guy?" Cassie complained. "He just shows up at the door and expects us to take him in."

"You said Mom was happy to see him."

"I guess, but there's no way I'm going back home until he's gone. I called Maggie and she said I could stay with her."

It seemed odd that Reginald had just shown up the way he had. While his presence concerned me, it also gave me an opportunity to try to find out more about him. Mom was marrying this guy in less than four weeks; we were running out of time to figure out exactly what his deal was.

"Did he happen to mention why he showed up?" I asked.

"No. I don't know. Maybe. He knocked on the door, Mom opened it, he yelled 'surprise,' and she threw herself into his arms. That was about the time I fled upstairs. I didn't come down until you came to get me. You know what's strange?"

"What?"

"He didn't have any luggage with him."

"Maybe it was in his car."

"Yeah, I guess it could have been. Grrr," Cassie growled in frustration. "That guy makes me so nuts. I can't tolerate the thought of having to sit at the same table with him for Thanksgiving, and don't even get me started on how he's going to ruin Christmas."

"I have to say I agree."

"The guy is just so weird. And he dyed his hair. I mean really: How vain can you get?"

"Mom dyes her hair," I pointed out.

"That's totally different. Why are you sticking up for him?"

"I'm not." The last time I saw Reginald his hair had been dark brown. "What color did he dye it?"

"Blond. A really light blond that makes him look younger. Do you remember if he said how old he is? When we met him before he had some gray in his hair, but he looked a lot younger last night."

"I don't remember him mentioning his age. I guess he could be younger than Mom, but I doubt he'd be that much younger. She's not really the type to be a cougar."

Of course based on her behavior at the naughty store, maybe she was *exactly* the sort to want a younger man. This whole thing was totally freaking me out. Cassie didn't know about the odd things Finn had discovered concerning the man's identity and I thought it was best not to say anything to her now. She was already pretty stressed out. Knowing that the guy who was going to marry our mother was a ghost without an identity might actually put her over the edge, so I decided to change the subject.

"Did Maggie tell you Haley is staying at her place too?"

"Yeah, she told me. That'll be cool. I like Haley and it'll be nice to have someone a little closer to my age to talk to."

"It's a good thing Maggie has a lot of bedrooms."

"It really is. You should come and spend the night one night. I know you live close by, but it would be fun to have you and me and Maggie and Haley and Siobhan all together. It'll be like a slumber party."

"I just might do that. Right now, though, I'm going to drop you and then go get ready for work. I have a feeling we're going to have another busy day."

When I arrived at Coffee Cat Books the place was packed. I grabbed my pink apron and jumped in to help our new hire, Roni, behind the coffee bar. Destiny and Tara both had their hands full with customers looking for books and souvenirs to take home.

"Deputy Finnegan came by earlier," Roni informed me. "He wanted to talk to you about something. He said for you to call him when you got in. He tried your cell but you didn't pick up."

My cell was in my backpack, which I'd tossed in the trunk of my car when I went to pick up Cassie and her luggage. I wouldn't have heard it ring and I hadn't thought to check my messages in my rush to get to work.

"Thanks. I'll call him as soon as things clear out a bit. Has it been this busy all morning?" I poured steamed milk into the cup marked "latte" before starting the next order.

"Pretty much. I didn't realize it would be this busy during the week. I expected it to be busy on Saturday, which it was, but I really thought there would be a lot of downtime today, being that it's a Monday and all."

"I guess summer really has arrived."

"By the way, I know who put the tracking device in your backpack," Tara called.

"Who?"

"Billy Flynn."

"Billy?" Billy was a twelve-year-old who had a tendency to get into trouble, but I couldn't come up with a single reason why he would want me dead. "Did he say why?"

"He said he was hanging out near the ferry terminal asking tourists for handouts when some old guy came up to him and gave him twenty bucks to sneak in and put the compact in your makeup case. The man told him that you were friends and the compact was just a funny gag. He thought the powder turned black when you put it on your face."

"Does Finn know?" I asked.

"Yeah, he knows. He talked to Billy, but you know him. He wasn't very helpful with a description."

"That's probably what Finn wants to talk to me about."

"Yeah, probably."

When things slowed down a bit I went into the office to call Finn. I'd thought he just wanted to tell me about the compact, but he'd really called to say he'd spoken to Val, who had remembered what it was she'd come to tell me that day in the store.

"Val was getting ready to leave the party and walked out onto the patio to say good-bye to anyone who was still there. She saw Daisy facedown in the pool and Alex passed out in the lounge chair. That's when she took the photo on her phone," Finn informed me. "She was about to head over to check on Alex—Daisy was obviously dead—when she heard voices. She hid behind some shrubbery and watched as one of the men she'd seen with Daisy earlier in the evening sprayed blood all over Alex's shirt. Then he took a knife out of his pocket and placed it in Alex's hand. He checked Alex's pulse and left."

"So this proves Alex was framed."

"It docs. Alex has been released from jail and is in a safe house with Balthazar Pottage."

I let out a sigh of relief that Alex was both free from jail and safe. "What did Val do after she saw the man spray Alex with blood?"

"As I said, she hid until she saw the man leave. I asked why she didn't call 911 right away and she said she hadn't been a hundred percent sure the man hadn't seen her; he'd looked in her direction, so she panicked and left. She thought about calling 911 after she got home but she was terrified, so she never did. When she heard Alex was in jail for Daisy's murder she decided to tell someone what she'd seen."

"Which is why she came to see me," I realized.

"Exactly. When you were busy and asked her to come back she decided to go down the street to run an errand. One of the men she'd seen at the party that night was walking toward her, so she ducked into the opening between Main Street and the alley. Then she pulled her cell out of her pocket to call 911 but dropped it. The man was at the entrance to the space where she was hiding and she panicked and ran toward the alley. Someone hit her on the head as she emerged from between the buildings; she doesn't remember who. She assumes it was the other man at the party. She got the idea the two of them were partners."

"Could she identify either of them?"

"I showed her the photo of Jimmy Gregory and she confirmed he was one of them. She gave us a description of the other one, but she didn't remember his name. She agreed to work with a sketch artist from Seattle, so we'll see what they come up with."

"Val is still staying with her friend?" I confirmed.

"I think she plans to stay in Seattle until we catch the guys we're looking for."

"I'm glad Val decided to share what she remembered. I hated to think of Alex sitting in jail. Now we just need to catch these creeps." I leaned back in the chair I was sitting in. I felt like things were finally beginning to come together. "How's Brittany doing?"

"Better. She should be released from the hospital later today. I wanted to set her up with some protection, but she's totally in denial. She insists she left the party before Daisy was killed so she doesn't know a thing. She's sure her accident was just an accident."

"Did you find any sort of GPS device in her car or on her person?"

"No. I suppose it *is* possible it really was just an accident, but I don't think so. How well do you know Brittany?"

"Not well, but I'm happy to talk to her if that's what you're getting out. Let me know when she's released from the hospital and I'll go over to her house to see what I can find out."

"Hang on."

I paused and waited while Finn said something to someone in the background.

"Sorry. The mail carrier was dropping off the mail," Finn explained.

"Not a problem. Did you ever get any information on Reginald? Apparently he showed up at my mom's house last night. Cassie said Mom had no idea he was coming, but of course she was thrilled to see him."

"I haven't been able to find anything on him, and no one by that name was registered on the cruise your mom took. He's obviously using an alias. If he's at your mom's, maybe we can use that to our advantage. See if you can get something with his fingerprints on it; we'll run them to see what comes up."

"Okay. I'll go over there today to try to get something. In the meantime, let me know if you find anything else. This entire situation has me worried."

"Yeah," Finn agreed, "me too. I've never even met the guy and I already don't like him. By the way, did Tara tell you we found out who put the compact in your backpack?"

"Yeah, she told me it was Billy. Do you have any idea who paid him to do it?"

"His vague description was pretty useless, but my money is on one of our thugs. His general description fits. I want you to promise me you'll be careful until we catch these guys."

"I promise."

Later that afternoon I headed toward Harthaven to pay Brittany a visit. I thought about calling ahead, but I wasn't sure she'd agree to see me and I figured it would be harder to say no to my face. Luckily, she answered the door herself when I rang the bell.

"I had a feeling you might be by." Brittany stepped aside and let me enter her home. "I've already told Deputy Finnegan everything I know, which isn't much."

"I know; I spoke to him. It's just that I honestly feel you may be in danger, and if something happens to you and I didn't at least try to change your mind about protective custody I'd never forgive myself."

"I know everyone thinks my accident was intentional, but why would anyone want to kill me? I don't know anything. Really."

"Finn told you the guardrail where you went over had been tampered with?"

"He did, but do you know how incredibly perfect someone would have to time it to swerve into my lane at that exact spot on the highway? Even if they were waiting around the bend for me, they'd have to know my speed and braking pattern to predict the exact moment I would be in that exact spot."

Brittany had a point. It would have had to have been a very carefully orchestrated plan. The fact that Val was attacked could have been the result of someone following her and then waiting for an opportunity, but even if Brittany was being tracked it would be hard to predict the precise moment when she'd be in a position to go through that exact guardrail. Unless more than one had been tampered with...I'd go by to check when I was done there, but for the moment I'd go along with Brittany in the hope that she'd tell me what she did know.

"Okay, I get what you're saying. Maybe it was an accident. But even if that's true is it okay if I ask you a few questions?"

"Sure. I guess."

"Why do you think Nick asked you to the party that night?"

"I don't know. He seemed to need warm bodies and wasn't being picky. I'm not rich like most of the people who go to those parties, but I'd been to a few and Nick and I knew each other."

"So the usual partygoers—where did they come from?"

"Somewhere on the mainland. Most of the time a bunch of rich men and women in their twenties all arrive on a yacht that ties up on Alex's dock. The parties tend to last two or three days and everyone who comes stays the entire time. If you haven't been to a seventy-two-hour party you're really missing something."

I doubted that would be something I'd ever want to experience but didn't say as much.

"Had anything odd happened at any of the previous parties you'd attended?"

"No, not really. I mean, everyone was drinking and doing drugs the entire time, so there were some weird things like random hookups in strange places and a few trips that weren't as fun as you might imagine, but no one died, if that's what you're asking."

"And after? Did you maintain friendships or stay in contact with any of the partygoers after everyone left and returned home?"

"There was this one girl who tried to get a bunch of us together to talk to the cops. She swore she was being blackmailed and needed other people who were at the party to testify as to what went on, but I didn't want the hassle, so I told her that I didn't know anything and wasn't interested in being a witness."

Not knowing anything and not wanting to be involved seemed to be a pattern for Brittany. If her accident really wasn't an accident I wondered why she of all people would be targeted. Maybe her trip off the cliff and into the sea really was a case of being in the wrong place at the wrong time.

"Who was still at the party when you left?" I asked.

"Nick, Daisy, Alex, Stephanie, Eric, Val. I think that's it. Oh, there were these two older guys. I'm not sure if they were still there or not."

"Had you seen them at any of the previous parties?"

"I'd never seen them before and haven't seen them since. Now, if you'll excuse me, I really need to rest."

"Certainly." I stood up. "Thank you for your time."

Brittany didn't respond as she closed the door behind me.

Well, that appeared to have been a waste of time. Either Brittany really didn't know anything or she just wasn't talking. I decided to head over to Shell Beach to look at the guardrails near the one Brittany had crashed into. Sure enough, there were several others before and after the one she'd plunged through that had likewise been tampered with. That was all the proof I needed to return to my first theory: someone had tried to kill Brittany.

Maybe Finn had managed to track down the two men no one other than Daisy seemed to know. I texted him to see if he was still in his office. He was, so I headed in that direction.

"I have good news and bad news," Finn began when I walked through the door.

"Hit me with the good news."

"I managed to track down Jimmy Gregory. He's on his way to lockup."

"That's wonderful news. Did he confess to killing Daisy?"

"No, but he did confess to helping the second guy frame Alex. He said killing Daisy was all on the man he was with."

"Would he give you the man's name?"

"He said he'd recently gotten out of prison and was working as a bouncer at one of the dive bars on the north shore. This guy who only identified himself as Rory walked up to him and gave him five grand to go to a party with him. Apparently Rory wanted Gregory to act as a sort of bodyguard. Gregory agreed, but when they got to the party he found out Rory wanted to mess with a bunch of the kids who were there. He helped to move Nick's body and to bring Alex down to the pool from his bedroom upstairs after they were drugged, and he even admitted to spraying blood on Alex's shirt, but he swears he didn't kill or drug anyone himself."

"So either Gregory is lying and we have our killer or he isn't and we still don't have the man responsible for all this."

"I checked Gregory's story out with the owner of the bar where he worked and he said he didn't notice who Gregory left with that night, but he had been there and he had left early."

"So what now?"

"Hope that Val can give the sketch artist a good enough description so we at least can nail down who it is we're looking for."

"I have news too," I said and shared my conversation with Brittany and my confirmation that several of the guardrails had been tampered with. Finn admitted he should have thought to check that himself and assured me he'd follow up and make sure the rails were repaired before someone else went plunging into the sea.

Chapter 13

I headed home after work to let Max out and to feed him and Ebenezer. Haley came by to play with Max on the lawn and I invited her to come for a walk with us. The rain had stopped and the clouds had cleared, leaving in their wake a beautiful summer day.

"So are you enjoying your stay so far?" I asked conversationally.

"So much. I love being here. I wish I could live here all the time."

"I'm sure your dad would miss you."

"Yeah," Haley said with a lack of conviction in her voice.

"Is there something going on at home?"

Haley shrugged. "Not really. It's just that my dad has started dating again."

"And you aren't sure how you feel about that?"

Haley picked up a stick and threw it into the waves. She smiled as Max ran in after it. "I guess it's okay that Dad wants to go on dates. My aunt told me it's natural for him to want to move on now that Mom is gone. She was sick for a long time, so I guess I can see why he wants to be happy again. It's just that I feel like he's cheating on Mom when I see him with other women."

"I guess that's a natural way to feel too."

"Dad doesn't think so. Every time I try to talk to him about it he gets mad and tells me that you can't cheat on a woman who's dead. I guess he's right, technically, but I don't like the women he brings around. They aren't like Mom at all."

"What do you mean?" I watched as Haley took the stick from Max and tossed it back into the waves.

"Mom was, you know, momish. She baked cookies and helped at my school. At least before she got sick. She always had a hug and a smile for me. The women my dad has been dating are all young and giggly. It's like the only thing that's important to them is going out and having a good time. There isn't a single person Dad has dated who would make a good mother. My aunt says not to worry. She thinks Dad's just having fun with these women and isn't necessarily going to marry any of them. I worry, though, that he'll fall in love and then I'll be stuck with a mother who isn't all that much older than me."

Max came running toward us through the waves. He splashed water on both of us, making Haley laugh. I watched as she chased him into the waves, looking happy and carefree, the way a thirteen-year-old should be. She'd had a tough few years and I really hoped that by the time she went home at the end of the summer her dad would be ready to settle down and begin dating a woman who would be a good wife *and* a good mother.

When we got back to Maggie's property Haley went inside to shower and change after getting soaked in the waves and I went into the cabin to check on Ebenezer and feed both my furry friends. Cody was working late that evening and I wasn't sure he was going to make it by. I'd overheard Finn and Siobhan making plans for dinner that evening and Tara had another date with her mystery man, so I made myself a sandwich and took it out onto the deck.

I thought about what Haley had said about feeling like her father was cheating on her mother by dating other women. I had to ask myself if I didn't have similar feelings clouding my opinion of Reginald. I'd like to think my dislike and mistrust of the man was based strictly on my impression of him, not some deeply held jealousy, but Reginald was the first man Mom had dated and I supposed it wouldn't be too far off base to say I felt Mom was better off without any man in her life if it couldn't be Dad.

"Hey, Cait." Cassie walked up and sat down next to me.

"Hey, Cassie. Are you all settled in?"

"Yeah. Maggie is always great and Haley is fun. I wondered if you could do me a huge favor."

"Probably. What is it?"

"I left my charger at the house and my phone is almost dead. Siobhan is out and Maggie is working late, so I wondered if you'd mind going over and getting it for me. If my phone dies I'll be totally cut off from my life."

"I'm not busy. I guess I can run over there. Where is it?"

"Plugged into the wall next to my nightstand." Cassie hugged me. "Thanks. You're the best sister ever."

Receiving a hug from my angsty teenage sister made any inconvenience totally worth it. I took Max and Ebenezer inside, got in the car, and headed toward Harthaven. Part of me wished I didn't have to deal with the unpleasant Mr. Pendergrass—or whatever his real name was—and part of me welcomed the chance to check on my mother. I wished Aiden was home from fishing. I was worried about Mom being alone in the house with Reginald. If Finn wasn't able to find out more about him on the sly, at some point we were all going to have to sit my mother down to have a talk with her. There was no way I wanted her marrying a man who seemed to be surrounded by red flags on all sides.

When I pulled up I noticed a black sedan in the drive. I was hoping Mom would be home alone so that I could talk to her, but apparently my wish wasn't to be granted. I opened the front door and let myself in as I had so many times before. "Hey, Mom, it's Cait," I called.

"In the kitchen, sweetheart."

I headed to the kitchen to find Mom alone.

"Whatever brings you by today? After the fit Cassie had I didn't think I'd see any of my children until the wedding."

I could see Mom was hurt by our attitudes toward her one and only love, but I really didn't think I had it in me to fake my feelings toward the guy.

"Cassie forgot her phone charger. I just popped over to get it. Any idea how long Reginald will be staying?"

"I'm not really sure. He didn't say. To be honest, I had no idea he was coming. I'm thrilled he's here, I really am, but I have so much to do to get ready for the wedding."

"Well, now that he's here he can help you."

"Oh, I can't bother him with things like cake and bouquets. He's a busy man. In fact, he's upstairs right now, trying to figure out how to merge our accounts."

"I thought you were going to wait for Aiden to get back before doing that."

"I was. I don't know anything about all this financial stuff, but Reginald seemed to think he could manage to do what needed to be done without Aiden's help as long as he had my social security number and some other personal information. If he can manage without Aiden's help that's all the better. Aiden hasn't been a fan of my intention to marry Reginald. The last time Reginald was here I really thought the two of them might come to blows."

Okay, this was bad. Really bad. I needed to grab Cassie's charger and then figure out a way to get hold of Aiden. If nothing else, maybe Finn could block the transfer of my mother's life savings before it was too late.

"What are you doing here?" Reginald walked into the kitchen just as Mom was slipping the casserole she was making into the oven. Cassie was right; he did look a lot younger than the first time I'd met him.

"I live here."

"Not anymore."

"All my children are welcome at any time," Mom said mildly. "This will always be their home."

"Until we sell it," Reginald pointed out.

"Yes, until then."

"I called a Realtor. He'll be by tomorrow afternoon to do the paperwork and put up a sign," Reginald informed Mom.

I noticed her frown. "Mom isn't going to put the house up for sale until after the wedding," I interjected.

"There's no reason to wait. The market is at its peak. Best to act now."

"I'm sorry, but I'm going to have to insist that she wait." I tried to look and act intimidating, but I don't think the tall man was afraid of a teeny, tiny woman.

"You're just a child. You can't possibly know what's best for your mother. I've been a very successful businessman for a lot of years. I suggest you butt out."

"Please don't fight," Mom fretted. "Cait is right; I would like Aiden to be here when we list the house. He's taken care of my finances since his father died. I trust him to know what's best."

Reginald looked like he wanted to argue but didn't say anything else. I was certain he was just waiting for me to leave so he could work his magic on my mom, convincing her to list the house right away. There was no way I was going to let that happen. I'd move back into the house so I could keep an eye on things if I had to.

"How's your investigation going, dear?" Mom asked in an attempt, I was sure, to change the subject.

"It's going okay. I think we're narrowing things down."

"That's good." Mom turned and looked at Reginald. "Did you hear we had a murder on the island?"

"I had heard, but I wasn't aware Caitlin was a cop."

"I'm not a cop, but I do help out. In fact, once we ID—" I paused when my phone dinged to indicate I had a text. I paused to look at the message from Finn, which included a sketch artist's rendering of the second older man. He not only looked familiar but he looked an awful lot like Reginald. I looked up and the instant our eyes met, I knew he'd realized I recognized who he really was.

"You just couldn't leave things alone." Reginald pulled out a gun.

"You killed Daisy and tried to kill Alex, Nick, Val, and Brittany. Why?"

"Whatever is going on?" Mom cried.

I grabbed my mother's arm and pulled her around so that she was standing behind me. "Who are you?"

"Reginald Pendergrass, your future stepdaddy."

"Over my dead body."

"Not an issue for me." Reginald raised the gun and pointed it at my head.

"Reginald, what are you doing?" Mom cried from behind me. "Did you kill that girl like Cait said?"

He rolled his eyes. "Of course I killed her. What did you think was going on here? Geez, you're daft. Now, both of you are going to slowly turn around and head toward the basement before my trigger finger gets itchy."

I wanted to argue, but there was no doubt in my mind that Reginald wouldn't hesitate to shoot both Mom and me, so I took her arm and whispered for her to go along quietly. Once we were in the basement Reginald told me to toss my cell phone into the hallway, and then he closed and locked the door behind him. I could hear him moving furniture, most likely Mom's hutch, which he was using to block the door so we couldn't escape.

"He's just going to leave us down here?" Mom looked as if she was in shock.

"I wish." There was no way he was leaving us alive. I had to think and I had to think fast.

"I don't understand what's happening." Mom stood in the middle of the basement, her face white as a sheet.

I pulled her into my arms and hugged her tight. "I'm sorry. I know this whole thing is unbelievable, but Reginald isn't who he told you he was. Right now I need to figure out a way to get us out of here. I need you to stand right here and let me think. I'll explain everything later."

I could hear him moving around upstairs. I could hear a lot of banging around; he seemed to be going through cupboards. After a few minutes I heard him leave the house. I momentarily let out the breath I'd been holding. Maybe he *was* just going to leave us down here and go away, and we'd only have to wait until someone found us. Then I heard him return to the kitchen and resume his banging around. The noise he was making was quickly followed by the unmistakable smell of gasoline. Oh God; he was going to burn down the house with us in it.

"We need to get out of here," I said to Mom. "And we need to get out fast."

Think, Cait, think. I looked around the basement. There had to be something I could use to get us out of this mess. I didn't have my phone and my mom didn't carry one. I didn't think calling out for help would work. In fact, it just might make Reginald work faster.

I knew that on the other side of the wood-paneled wall was a crawl space that ran the entire length of the house. All I needed to do was make a hole in the wall large enough to crawl through; then I could crawl under the house until I reached the access point at the back. I looked around for something to use to make the hole. I was afraid that if I tried to punch one with a solid object Reginald would hear me, but I really felt that was my only option. I was debating what to do when I began to smell the very distinct odor of smoke. I picked up an old bat someone had discarded at some point and hit the wall with all my might. The walls were thick, so it took me several minutes to punch a hole large enough for us to crawl through.

It was dark under the house and the smoke, which had started in the kitchen, was already beginning to fill the crawl space. This was looking like a really bad idea, but it had been the only one I had.

"Surely you aren't going to crawl through that little hole?" Mom asked.

"We both are. I'll go first, but you have to promise to follow me."

"But it's dark. Who knows what's down there?"

"Whatever it is can't be as bad as staying here."

I crawled through and tried to get my bearings. It was already getting dark outside, so there wasn't much light coming through the small openings under the house. I could hear fire engines in the distance, but they didn't know we were down here, so no one would come look here until it was much too late.

"Come on, Mom. We need to do this now."

"I can't. The space is too small."

"Put your arms through first. I'll pull you out."

Mom did as I asked, and although it took quite a bit of effort, I managed to pull her through. The smoke was getting thick. We needed to move fast. The problem was that without any light, it made it close to impossible to figure out exactly where the crawl space was. I closed my eyes and tried to remember. Danny and I had played down here as kids. I used to know my way around even with my eyes closed.

"Follow me," I instructed Mom as I got into position to crawl toward where I hoped I remembered the crawl space was.

"I can't see anything."

"Just keep one hand next to my foot at all times. I'll go slowly so you can keep up, but we need to go now."

My lungs burned as the smoke thickened. I could hear timbers crashing overhead. Reginald had obviously used some type of accelerant for the fire to burn so hot so fast. It wouldn't be long before the smoke would render us unconscious.

Mom coughed. "I can't go on."

"Just a little farther. We're almost there."

"You go. Save yourself. I can't make it."

"Like hell. We both make it or neither of us does; now crawl."

I was on the verge of giving up myself when I felt some fresh air. "Just a few more yards. Come on, Mom, you can do it."

When I reached the entrance to the crawl space I suddenly remembered the screen Aiden had put across the opening to prevent squirrels from getting in. I wanted to cry. I didn't know if I had the strength left to kick away the screen. It was so hot. I couldn't breathe.

"Why'd we stop?" Mom asked.

"We're here. I forgot about the screen."

Mom began to pray out loud. I kicked at the screen, but it wouldn't give away. I was on the verge of blacking out when I swear I saw Ebenezer on the other side of the screen. Seconds later, Cody was kneeling next to him.

"Cait?"

"We're here."

It only took Cody a few seconds to remove the screen and pull me and Mom to safety. Mom was unconscious, but emergency personnel had arrived by then. They strapped an oxygen mask to her face and took her to the ambulance.

"Cait." Cassie ran over and hugged me. "I'm so glad you're okay. Mom?"

"In the ambulance." I hugged Cassie one more time. "Go. Be with her. I'm fine."

Cassie did as I suggested and I saw her wave just before the doors to the ambulance closed and they took off toward the hospital.

"How'd you know we needed you?" I asked Cody.

"When I arrived at your place Cassie was there, and she told me Ebenezer was flipping out, acting crazy. I knew a crazy cat meant my crazy girlfriend had gotten herself into a bind once again. Cassie told me that you'd come here to get her phone charger so we headed this way. When we heard the sirens we drove faster. Ebenezer led me right to you."

"Remind me to buy extra salmon treats on the way home. That cat deserves a whole bag."

"A whole bag might make him sick, but maybe a few extra are in order."

I walked around to the front of the house and watched as my childhood home went up in flames. I couldn't bear the knowledge that my own children would never slide down the same banister I had, or that I'd never again sit in my dad's big leather chair that had been molded to his form after years upon years of use. I cried, remembering the notch marks on five bedroom walls where Mom had measured our growth from one year to the next, and I mourned the loss of the priceless Christmas ornaments that had been handed down for five generations.

"Finn and Siobhan are here," Cody whispered in my ear.

Siobhan ran toward me, tears running down her face. "Mom?"

"On her way to the hospital. Cassie is with her. She's okay. Just some smoke inhalation."

"What happened?"

"It's a long story." I looked at Finn. "You have to stop Reginald from leaving the island. He killed Daisy and he tried to kill us."

"We'll get him. He can't have gotten far. We've got volunteers at all the marinas and the ferry station. He won't get away."

Chapter 14

Sunday, July 3

"I get dibs on the last of the potato salad," Danny claimed as all the Harts enjoyed a meal together at the community picnic.

"Then I get the last brownie," Cassie countered.

It filled my heart with happiness and gratitude that we were all together and that, other than the loss of a home we'd all loved, we'd all survived and in many ways were closer than ever. Aiden was home from his most recent fishing trip and was staying with Danny, and Mom was staying with Maggie for the time being. At first I'd thought that was a terrible idea, but it seemed she was enjoying her time with Maggie, Siobhan, Cassie, and Haley, and they in turn were enjoying her now that she was no longer under the spell of the man whose name, we'd found out, was actually Bert Dingby. Bert was a con artist from way back who'd currently been working a scam in which he'd find older, vulnerable women to seduce into giving him their life savings. Luckily, we'd stopped him before he could get his hands on any more of Mom's than he already had.

As promised, Finn had managed to track down Bert and even gotten him to confess to not only being the mastermind behind the blackmail scheme involving wealthy twentysomethings but to killing Daisy, drugging Nick and Alex, assaulting Val, and running Brittany off the road. It seemed he'd gotten the idea when he visited my mother and found out about Alex. He'd hired Daisy and Nick to help him run what could have been the perfect scam if Daisy hadn't started to have second thoughts. He was currently in jail, where Finn assured me he'd be going to prison for a very long time.

Alex and Balthazar Pottage had joined us for the picnic that kicked off a day filled with holiday fun including a kiddie carnival and a fireworks display. Haley looked like she was having the time of her life and even Cassie was letting a bit of her inner child come through as she knocked Finn off his pedestal at the dunking cage.

"Siobhan and I have an announcement to make," Finn said after standing up. He pulled Siobhan to her feet.

"We're getting married." Siobhan's entire face shone with happiness as she waved her ring finger in front of us.

Everyone jumped up to hug everyone else and to congratulate the happy couple. I glanced at Mom, and there was nothing but joy on her face. I was worried she'd mourn the loss of the man she'd thought she'd loved, but she seemed to have bounced back from the temporary insanity that was her engagement with grace and thankfulness for all she hadn't lost.

"I'm glad Mr. Parsons was able to join us today," I said to Cody. "It seems like he's having a good time."

"He is, but not as good a time as Maggie and Father Kilian. Is something going on that I don't know about?"

I looked over to where Maggie was admiring Siobhan's ring and Father Kilian was gazing at her with an expression of unmasked love. I'm sure no one realized what was going on other than Maggie's best friend, Marley, who had a confused expression on her face. Maggie and Father Kilian were going to have to be more careful if they didn't want their secret getting out.

"I'll tell you about it later."

Cody laced his fingers with mine. "It's nice your family is all together."

I turned and kissed him briefly on the mouth. "Do you want to take a walk?"

"Sure. If you'd like."

Cody and I got up and told the others we were going to stretch our legs and would be back in a few minutes.

"It's exciting news about Finn and Siobhan," Cody commented.

"It is." I smiled. "I always hoped they'd find their way back to each other. Finn has been such a huge part of my life for so long, he feels like a brother."

Cody looked like he was going to say something when I noticed something in the distance. "Look over there."

Cody glanced in the direction I was pointing. "Ariel?"

"I think so. Everyone who's tried to catch her so far has failed. We need to be stealthy."

"I think it might be easier than it seems," Cody commented as Ebenezer walked across the grass toward the dog that just stood and watched it approach.

"How in the heck did he...never mind." I was going to ask how the cat had gotten from my cabin to the park, but I'd learned just to accept the gifts cats brought to my life without questioning them. I watched as Ebenezer led Ariel across the lawn to where Cody and I were standing.

"Are you ready to go home?" I asked.

Apparently he was. He followed Ebenezer, Cody, and me to Cody's car and jumped right in. Cody followed my directions to the house Rosalyn's dad had rented. I picked up the small dog and walked up the steps to the front door, with Cody and Ebenezer following behind.

"Ariel," Rosalyn screamed when she opened the door. The little dog squirmed out of my arms and ran to greet her human. Tears were streaming down Rosalyn's face. She hugged Ariel and turned to look at Ebenezer. "Thank you, Ebenezer. I knew you'd find her."

Cody and I just looked at each other. "You know Ebenezer?" I asked.

"He visited me in my dream. He promised to bring Ariel home and he did."

I picked Ebenezer up and cuddled him to my chest, then held his face to mine. "One of these days you're going to have to tell me how you do that."

"You aren't supposed to understand miracles," Rosalyn commented. "You're just supposed to believe in them."

I smiled. "I guess you're right. I'm happy Ebenezer found Ariel for you."

"Thank you for your help too."

"Anytime."

"Oh, and congratulations," Rosalyn said to Cody and me when we turned to walk away.

"Congratulations? For what?" I asked.

"Ebenezer told me that one day you two are going to have a little girl named Rosalyn who has long brown hair and big blue eyes just like me."

Recipes by Kathi Daley

Cheesy Chicken Casserole
Cheesy White Chicken Enchiladas
Twice Baked Potato Casserole
Fettuccine Alfredo

Recipes by Readers

Tropical Treat Bread—submitted by Vivian Shane
Strawberry Yogurt Pie—submitted by Nancy Farris
No Bake Tropical Cheesecake—submitted by Joanne Kocourek
Mom's Chicken and Cheese Casserole—submitted by Elaine Robinson

Cheesy Chicken Casserole

1 box (16 oz.) penne pasta
4 chicken breasts, cooked and cubed
1 can Campbell's Cream of Cheddar soup
1 can Campbell's Nacho Cheese soup
(you can use two cans of either if you like
your casserole more or less spicy)
2 cups cheddar cheese, shredded
1 cup Parmesan cheese, grated
1 jar (16 oz.) Alfredo sauce (any brand)
¾ cup milk
1 cup cashews (or more if you'd like)
Salt and pepper to taste
Cheddar cheese crackers

Boil pasta according to directions on box
(10–12 minutes).

Meanwhile, mix cooked and cubed
chicken, soups, cheeses, Alfredo sauce,
milk, cashews, and salt and pepper
together in a large bowl.

Drain pasta when tender and add to
chicken mixture. Stir until well mixed.

Pour into a greased 9 x 13 baking pan. Top with crumbled cheddar cheese crackers.

Bake at 350 degrees for 30 minutes.

Cheesy White Chicken Enchiladas

Preheat oven to 350 degrees. Spray 9 x 13 baking dish with nonstick spray.

Mix in a bowl:

3 large chicken breasts, cooked and cubed
1 cup sour cream
8 oz. diced green chiles (Ortega)

Fill 8 medium flour tortillas with chicken filling.

Sauce:
In a medium saucepan combine:
1 stick butter, melted over medium heat
4 oz. cream cheese, added to melted butter and stirred until smooth
1 cup heavy whipping cream, stirred until blended
1½ cups grated Parmesan, stirred in slowly to avoid lumps

Pour over tortillas and top with 16 oz. Monterey Jack cheese, grated.

Bake uncovered at 350 degrees for 20–25 minutes. Broil for a few minutes to brown.

Twice Baked Potato Casserole

5 medium to large russet potatoes, baked
10 pieces bacon, cooked crispy and crumbled
2 cups cheddar cheese, shredded
1 cup Parmesan cheese, grated
1 pt. sour cream
½ cup green onion, chopped
Salt
Pepper

Either dice whole cooked potatoes or scoop out inner potato and discard skin. Combine with remaining ingredients. Transfer to greased baking dish. Bake at 350 degrees for 50 minutes until bubbly and lightly browned.

Fettuccine Alfredo

Melt 1 stick butter (real butter, no substitutions) in saucepan over medium heat.

When melted add:
½ 8 oz. pkg. cream cheese
2 cups heavy whipping cream

Stir until cream cheese is completely dissolved.

Slowly add:
1½ cups Parmesan cheese, grated (the good stuff)
1 cup Romano cheese grated (add slowly; don't let it clump)

Stir until smooth.

Add:
1 tsp. ground nutmeg
½ tsp. garlic powder

Add salt and pepper to taste

Note: if you like your sauce thicker you can add additional Parmesan and if you like it thinner you can add additional cream.

Pour over fettuccine, tortellini, or any other pasta (fresh from the refrigerator section is best).

Tropical Treat Bread

Submitted by Vivian Shane

This yummy bread tastes like carrot cake but with a coconut twist! I always try to fool myself that I'm only making this as a way to get more fruit and veggies into my diet….

3 cups flour
2 cups sugar
1 tsp. baking soda
1 tsp. cinnamon
¾ tsp. salt
3 eggs
1½ cups carrots
¼ cup coconut, flaked
¼ cup golden raisins
8 oz. can unsweetened crushed pineapple, drained
1 cup vegetable oil (I have also substituted applesauce for the oil)
1 cup pecans
2 tsp. vanilla

In a large bowl, combine flour, sugar, baking soda, cinnamon, and salt. In another bowl, beat the eggs. Add carrots, coconut, raisins, pineapple, vegetable oil, pecans, and vanilla and stir to combine. Stir this mixture into the dry ingredients until just moistened. Spoon into two greased and floured 8 x 4 x 2 loaf pans. Bake at 350 degrees for 65–75 minutes or until a toothpick inserted in center comes out clean. Cool in pan for 15 minutes, then remove and cool completely on wire rack.

I occasionally drizzle the top with some ready-made cream cheese frosting thinned down with milk to make it drizzle consistency.

Strawberry Yogurt Pie

Submitted by Nancy Farris

When I moved to Louisville in the early eighties I joined my local sorority alumni group to meet more people. They were all wonderful ladies who welcomed me with open arms and opened doors for me in the business community. One of my sisters served this dessert at one of our meetings and I've since adapted it in her honor in pink because she died from breast cancer. This is for you, Linda.

You can use any combination of Jell-O, yogurt, and fruit, but this is my favorite.

Crust:
In a skillet, melt ⅓ cup butter. Add ¾ cup of flour and ⅓ cup of chopped almonds and 2 tbs. honey or agave. Let cook for 3–4 minutes until light brown. Let cool for a few minutes, then press into a 9" pie plate.

Filling:

Put the following into a mixing bowl. Add 1 cup boiling water and stir until dissolved.
⅓ oz. pkg. strawberry Jell-O
½ cup sugar
½ tsp. salt
Let cool a few minutes, then add 8 oz. strawberry yogurt and 2 cups chopped fresh strawberries. Mix well and pour into pie crust. Chill until set.
One of my other favorite combinations is lemon Jell-O, vanilla yogurt, and fresh blueberries. There are so many combinations out there that you can adapt to your favorite flavors or the fruits in season.

No Bake Tropical Cheesecake

Submitted by Joanne Kocourek

A light dessert perfect for summer, when fresh fruit is abundant.

15 graham crackers (enough to cover bottom of 9 x 13 pan/dish)
Alternative option: Cut a store-bought angel food cake into cubes as the base
2–3 cups strawberries, thinly sliced (enough to cover bottom and top layer)
8 oz. cream cheese
1 cup milk
1 box instant vanilla or cheesecake pudding (4-serving size, regular, fat free, or sugar free)
1½ cups fresh pineapple fresh, finely chopped and drained (or drained, crushed pineapple)
8 oz. lemon yogurt (regular or fat free)
2 cups fresh whipping cream or Cool Whip (regular or low fat), divided

Line a 9 x 13 pan with a single layer of graham crackers (left whole, unless you need to break them to fit in the pan). Top with a single layer of sliced strawberries.

In the bowl of a stand mixer, beat cream cheese until smooth and fluffy. Add milk and pudding mix and beat until smooth, stopping to scrape down the sides if necessary.

Stir in pineapple and yogurt. Slowly stir in 1 cup of whipped topping.

Spread in the pan over the strawberries. Top with remaining cup of whipped topping.

Decorate with remaining strawberry slices.

Refrigerate at least 6–8 hours so that graham crackers can soften and become cakelike. It can be made ahead and frozen too.

Note: If desired, half of the strawberries can be chopped and folded into the mixture instead of layering on the graham cracker or angel food cake cube base.

Mom's Chicken and Cheese Casserole

Submitted by Elaine Robinson

Chicken and cheese casserole was one of my favorite meals my late mom use to cook. It brings back fond memories and good feelings.

1 bag noodles
1 cup cooked chicken (may use canned chicken)
1 can cream of mushroom soup
Bar of cheese

Cook noodles on stovetop; layer casserole dish with noodles, chicken, and cheese; add cream of mushroom soup; preheat oven to 350 degrees and cook for 60 minutes.

This dish is also yummy as a leftover.

Books by Kathi Daley

Come for the murder, stay for the romance.

Zoe Donovan Cozy Mystery:

Halloween Hijinks
The Trouble With Turkeys
Christmas Crazy
Cupid's Curse
Big Bunny Bump-off
Beach Blanket Barbie
Maui Madness
Derby Divas
Haunted Hamlet
Turkeys, Tuxes, and Tabbies
Christmas Cozy
Alaskan Alliance
Matrimony Meltdown
Soul Surrender
Heavenly Honeymoon
Hopscotch Homicide
Ghostly Graveyard
Santa Sleuth
Shamrock Shenanigans
Kitten Kaboodle
Costume Catastrophe – *August 2016*

Whales and Tails Cozy Mystery:

Romeow and Juliet
The Mad Catter
Grimm's Furry Tail
Much Ado About Felines
Legend of Tabby Hollow
Cat of Christmas Past
A Tale of Two Tabbies
The Great Catsby
Count Catula – *September 2016*
Cat of Christmas Present – *November 2016*

Seacliff High Mystery:

The Secret
The Curse
The Relic
The Conspiracy
The Grudge

Sand and Sea Hawaiian Mystery:

Murder at Dolphin Bay
Murder at Sunrise Beach
Murder at the Witching Hour – *September 2016*

Road to Christmas Romance:
Road to Christmas Past

Tj Jensen Paradise Lake
Pumpkins in Paradise – Sept. 2016
Snowmen in Paradise – Sept 2016
Bikinis in Paradise – Sept 2016
Christmas in Paradise – Sept 2016
Puppies in Paradise – Sept 2016
Halloween in Paradise – Sept 2016
Treasure in Paradise – April 2017

Kathi Daley lives with her husband, kids, grandkids, and Bernese mountain dogs in beautiful Lake Tahoe. When she isn't writing, she likes to read (preferably at the beach or by the fire), cook (preferably something with chocolate or cheese), and garden (planting and planning, not weeding). She also enjoys spending time on the water when she's not hiking, biking, or snowshoeing the miles of desolate trails surrounding her home.

Kathi uses the mountain setting in which she lives, along with the animals (wild and domestic) that share her home, as inspiration for her cozy mysteries.

Kathi is a top 100 mystery writer for Amazon and she won the 2014 award for both Best Cozy Mystery Author and Best Cozy Mystery Series.

She currently writes four series: Zoe Donovan Cozy Mysteries, Whales and Tails Island Mysteries, Sand and Sea Hawaiian Mysteries, and Seacliff High Teen Mysteries.

Giveaway:

I do a giveaway for books, swag, and gift cards every week in my newsletter, *The Daley Weekly*
http://eepurl.com/NRPDf

Other links to check out:
Kathi Daley Blog: publishes each Friday
http://kathidaleyblog.com
Webpage **www.kathidaley.com**
Facebook at Kathi Daley Books -
www.facebook.com/kathidaleybooks
Kathi Daley Teen –
www.facebook.com/kathidaleyteen
Kathi Daley Books Group Page –
https://www.facebook.com/groups/569578823146850/
E-mail - **kathidaley@kathidaley.com**
Goodreads:
https://www.goodreads.com/author/show/7278377.Kathi_Daley
Twitter at Kathi Daley@kathidaley -
https://twitter.com/kathidaley

Amazon Author Page -
https://www.amazon.com/author/ka thidaley
BookBub -
https://www.bookbub.com/authors/ kathi-daley
Pinterest -
http://www.pinterest.com/kathidale y/

53752737R00127

Made in the USA
Lexington, KY
18 July 2016